THE
COMMANDER

NEW YORK TIMES AND *USA TODAY* BESTSELLING AUTHOR

MELANIE MORELAND

MEN OF
HIDDEN JUSTICE

Dear Reader,

Thank you for selecting The Commander to read. Be sure to sign up for my newsletter for up to date information on new releases, exclusive content and sales. You can find the form here: https://bit.ly/MMorelandNewsletter

Before you sign up, add melanie@melaniemoreland.com to your contacts to make sure the email comes right to your inbox! **Always fun - never spam!**

My books are available in paperback and audiobook! You can see all my books available and upcoming preorders at my website.

The Perfect Recipe For **LOVE**

xoxo,

Melanie

The Commander by Melanie Moreland

Copyright © 2021 Moreland Books Inc.
Copyright ©1189468
ISBN Ebook 978-1-988610-79-5
Paperback 978-1-988610-82-5/978-1-988610-81-8
Audio 978-1-988610-83-2

MORELAND
BOOKS INC.

Edited by Lisa Hollett of Silently Correcting Your Grammar
Cover design by Karen Hulseman, Feed Your Dreams Designs
Cover Photography by Regina Wamba Photography
Cover content is for illustrative purposes only and any person depicted
on the cover is a model.

DEDICATION

For all of you who have embraced my Canadian Gray—
This is for you
For my Matthew—always
And to Karen
Who always wants more
And more
And more

Love you all

PRESENT DAY

Julian

I reached for a file, trying not to curse under my breath. Then I recalled I had a private office so I could curse all I wanted.

"Fucking paperwork," I snarled. "It never ends."

I picked up my coffee, cursing yet again when I realized the cup was empty. I punched the intercom, waiting until my secretary responded.

"Yes, sir?"

I managed to keep my voice civil. "Coffee, Anne. Now."

"Right away. A sandwich, perhaps?"

"Is it lunchtime?"

"It's two o'clock."

I shook my head in disbelief. The days passed in a rush of moments, it seemed.

It was a shame the nights dragged so badly.

"I would appreciate that."

I hung up before she could respond. She was an older woman, happy to have a job, not caring about the dull work she processed daily. She had no idea what really happened in the office behind her, and it was best kept that way. I had learned my lesson once.

Anne came in at ten, left at four, and when she wasn't typing or filing, getting me lunch or coffee, she kept herself busy. I didn't care. She was a cover, and it worked well for both of us.

An hour later, I finished signing all the papers, and I shoved them out of the way, running a hand over my eyes. I looked over at the sandwich sitting on the edge of my desk, the edges curling and drying, and I tapped the plate, knocking it into the garbage can.

My phone rang, and I answered it tersely.

"Julian Grayson."

"Yeah, Commander, it's Conrad Baines."

Conrad was one of my security men. An excellent ex-agent and happily working in another capacity for me—but he was on leave. "Conrad, what's up?"

"I'm here at the London airport, waiting to leave for our vacation."

I blinked, unsure what that had to do with me. "Okay."

"We like to fly out of here. Smaller than Toronto, you know? No crowds, no lineups."

"Yes, I understand," I said impatiently. I didn't really have time for idle chitchat about airports in Canada. But his next words hit me like a freight train.

"I saw her, Commander."

"Saw who?"

"Your wife."

My body locked down.

My wife. I hadn't heard those words in months.

"My ex, you mean," I said numbly, feeling the shock of his words. We weren't even technically divorced, but I let people think that way. It was easier.

I hadn't been able to find her since the day she'd walked out. It was as if she had disappeared. And for him to have spotted her?

What were the chances?

I realized he was still talking.

"The reason I noticed her, aside from the red hair, that is, was the fact that she had someone with her."

My stomach tightened.

She was with someone? Was that why she really left me?

"Oh?" I managed to get out.

"Yeah. She was carrying a baby. Like, a four-month-old baby. And the baby—she looked just like you. I'd recognize those eyes anywhere."

His words exploded in my head. They echoed and ricocheted around my brain, growing and expanding every second.

Wife.

Baby.

Four months.

She.

Eyes.

Looked like you.

I was on my feet in a second, standing so fast my chair hit the wall.

"Do you know what flight she's waiting for?"

"Same as ours. She's headed to the Maritimes." He rattled off a number.

"Keep her in your sight," I snarled. "Don't let her see you."

"Good thing the plane is late—"

"It's going to be a lot later. Sorry."

I slammed down the phone, not waiting for him to respond. I pressed another button, already speaking before the person answering finished his greeting.

"I need Flight WJ873, departing London, Ontario, grounded until I get there. Mechanical issue—whatever you need to say for it to stay on the ground. Keep the passengers calm and in the terminal."

I hung up again and made another call.

"I need a helicopter. Now."

THE BEGINNING

CHAPTER ONE

Julian

I rubbed my face, staring at the hidden cameras in the outer office. Five women were waiting to meet with me. All typical of the type of woman who applied for the job I'd posted. Late fifties, looking for something to fill in a few hours three days a week. Nothing difficult, strenuous, or exciting. Boring, actually. I purposely geared the job description that way to attract that age demographic. Labeled the description *secretary*, not assistant.

Joyce, my current secretary, was leaving after two years. She'd lasted longer than most but decided Florida and the sunshine held more promise than another dreary winter in Toronto. I couldn't really blame her, although I would miss her. She was quietly efficient, lacked any sort of motivation to "do more," and was just as happy sitting at her desk knitting yet another afghan for someone than to ask for additional tasks. Of which I had zero. So, she kept knitting, collecting her paycheck, and keeping the legitimate business of security I offered running smoothly. The phone was answered, invoices sent out, monies collected, and events scheduled. She did it well, so I had zero problem with the knitting.

In fact, I had two of her afghans myself. They were very soft.

I picked up the phone. "Send the first one in, Joyce," I instructed.

Four hours later, I stared at the résumés each woman left. They were all fine. Capable. One was actually perfect. Susan had accounting experience, knew how to run an office, was only looking for some time out of her house now that her husband had retired. That seemed to be the running theme with a lot of these women. She had informed me she could work ten to four, three days a week, and she didn't carry a cell phone, nor could she work weekends. I had assured her that was fine.

Any of them would fill in nicely for Joyce. And I knew, soon enough, they would get bored or move on once something else came along, and Elite Security would be a distant memory.

Exactly how I wanted it.

I stood, deciding I would think about it overnight and make a final decision tomorrow, although I was leaning toward Susan. She was the top candidate and would do well in the role. I told the agency I used not to send anyone else. I had enough to choose from.

I slipped on my jacket, straightening my sleeves, and grabbed my cell phone. I was going to head to the local bar and grab a late lunch. I had a full evening ahead of me.

But as I stepped into the outer office, the door leading to the hall burst open and a woman stumbled in. She was breathing hard, her hand pressed against her chest. Her eyes widened when she saw me, and I was stunned into silence.

She was in her late twenties. About ten years younger than me, I guessed. Average height, with full breasts and wide hips I glimpsed under her coat. But it was her hair that caught my attention. It streamed over her shoulders and down her back in a riotous mass of curls and spirals. And the color. Vivid copper with highlights of gold and brown woven in and catching the bright lights of the late-afternoon sun that filtered through the window.

Her cheeks were flushed, staining her creamy skin a dull pink and highlighting a scattering of freckles along the bridge of her nose and the tops of her cheekbones. Finally, I met her eyes. Bright sapphire blue met my stare, her gaze anxious.

"Am I too late?" she gasped out.

"Late?" I asked, confused. "I think you have the wrong office."

"For the secretarial job? Isn't this Elite Security?"

I gaped at her. She was looking for a job—*here*?

Absolutely not.

She spelled one word. Trouble. The exact kind of trouble I didn't need.

Yet before I could comprehend what I was doing, I swept out my arm.

"No, you're not too late. Come in."

I escorted her into my office, my hand hovering near her lower back, itching to touch her. Her head came to my shoulder, and when I inhaled, I could smell the scent of her incredible hair. As she moved, the strands brushed the back of my hand, and I had to forcibly stop myself from fisting it to find out if it was as soft as the curls felt briefly on my skin.

I waited until she was in front of my desk. "May I offer you anything?" I asked. "Water, coffee…?"

"Oh, a water would be great. I ran all the way here from the subway."

That explained the flush. I headed to the corner and pulled a bottle of water from the fridge, setting it down in front of her. I tried not to stare as she picked up the bottle and drank deeply, her throat moving in time with her swallows. The skin there was fair and delicate, faint blue lines of veins running under the surface, highlighting the paleness of her neck.

"Much better," she murmured, then removed her coat, revealing a simple shift dress. It clung to her curves, highlighting her breasts and hips, and showing off her neck and arms. I suspected it showed off her legs as well, but aside from dropping down to check, I had to keep my assumption private.

I indicated the chair. "Sit, please."

She did so gracefully, crossing her legs, and thanks to my glass-topped desk, confirming they were indeed shapely. She bent and pulled an envelope from her bag, handing it to me. I noted her low voice and serious expression.

"My résumé."

I accepted the envelope, our fingers brushing briefly. I tried not to start at the feeling of her skin against mine. Internally, I shook my head. I must be hungry since there was no other explanation as to why I was acting this way. Why I had even allowed her into my office. She wasn't the right type for this job.

She was far too… I glanced up at her, meeting her vivid blue gaze, then dropped my eyes back to the piece of paper I had pulled from the envelope. She was far too *everything* I avoided.

"I think there's been a mistake," I said.

"Is the job filled?" she asked, her voice rife with disappointment.

"Ah, no, but it's only part time. Clerical work—boring stuff."

"I'm good with that," she assured me.

"Filing, answering phones, sending invoices, scheduling jobs."

She nodded. "Fine."

I glanced back at her simple résumé. She was a university graduate. An art major. I had guessed her age right at twenty-eight. Had some office experience.

"The job is dull as dishwater," I stated honestly. "The agency sent you?"

"I begged them. They said I wasn't the right profile, but I wanted a shot. I'd do a good job for you, Mr.…ah,

Mr. Grayson." She paused. "You *are* Mr. Grayson, right?"

Hearing my name on her tongue made me realize two things. One, I liked it. And two, I had never introduced myself or even registered her name. I glanced at the top of the sheet of paper and cleared my throat.

"Forgive me, Miss Wells, for my lack of manners. Yes, I'm Julian Grayson." I looked back at the résumé. "Or is it Mrs. Wells? Ms.?"

"Miss or Ms. is fine. But I prefer Taliyah."

"Pretty name," I said before I could stop myself, secretly thrilled she had let me know she wasn't married.

She remained silent, but her cheeks flushed again.

"I keep things pretty casual here. Julian is fine," I replied. I was lying through my teeth. My secretaries always called me Mr. Grayson, but I wanted to hear her say my name.

"Julian," she repeated then offered me her first smile. It was tremulous but very appealing. "I would do a good job."

"I have no doubt you would, but why?" I asked her. "This job is going nowhere. There is nothing to reach for, no higher level to aspire to. You're rather young to dead-end yourself in a job like the one I'm offering."

Except to her.

I wasn't offering the job to her, I reminded myself.

She lifted her shoulders in an elegant shrug. "Because I have student debt to pay off. Because no one is hiring in my field. I can work here, also bartend on the weekends to make ends meet, pay my bills and still have some time to volunteer at galleries and museums to get my foot in the door," she stated honestly.

I liked her frankness.

"Bartend?" I questioned.

She nodded. "At 7&7. I do the night shifts on Friday and Saturday. Do you know it?"

"I do. It's close to my apartment."

It was a small bar, had a decent menu, and on occasion, I ate there, enjoying the buzz of the space after a long day. It was a bit rough around the edges, but the owner ran a clean place, and I had never heard much bad about it.

"You're a hard worker."

Again, she shrugged. "I do what I have to."

"Not much time for a social life," I said, fishing for more information.

"You need to have one to miss it, Julian," she replied.

I liked my name on her lips too much. I also liked knowing there was no one in her life. Internally, I frowned. I shouldn't care. I shouldn't even be thinking about this. She was all wrong for the job. She was too smart, too educated, and too damn young and attractive. I could only imagine how the security guys would react to her. How often I'd have to put the single ones in their place.

How distracting she would be to me with that hair and those mesmerizing eyes.

And her legs.

I didn't need those kinds of distractions.

"It's four days a week, six hours a day." I rattled off a salary I had never once paid before.

Her remarkable eyes widened. "The agency said three."

"Is four too much?"

"No, it's even better. And the salary is great."

I needed to stop this madness. "There have been lots of applicants."

The light that had started to glow in her eyes dimmed, and she swallowed. "I understand." She stood, extending her hand. "Thank you for your time, Mr. Grayson. My number is on my résumé if you want to get in touch."

She gathered her coat, slipping it over her shoulders. She turned and headed for the door, defeat in her posture.

I couldn't stand to see her walk away.

I couldn't have her here either.

My mind was at war. Logic lost.

"Ms. Wells, *Taliyah*, wait."

She turned, meeting my eyes, her gaze cautiously hopeful.

"A one-month trial. It's the best I can offer."

"I'll take it. You won't be disappointed."

But you might be, I thought. Then I spoke out loud.

"When can you start?"

CHAPTER TWO

Julian

I cursed myself the rest of the night. For the entire morning the next day. I knew I needed to withdraw the offer. To call and tell her I had made a mistake, even offer to help her find another job. But instead, I called the agency, removed the job listing, and paid them their fee. I liked working with them since they gave me people to choose from and I hired them directly once I made my decision. No more middleman. I liked to keep it simple that way.

Except, with my choice, I'd made this hire complicated.

Taliyah was going to be anything but easy. I already knew it.

Joyce looked shocked when I told her the new girl would be in the following Monday and she could show her the ropes. She glanced at the résumé, her eyebrows high.

"Twenty-eight? Younger than your usual secretaries, Mr. Grayson."

I wanted to run my finger under my suddenly tight collar, but I refrained. Instead, I straightened my shoulders. "She was well qualified, and I decided to go in a different direction. And she could start right away."

"So, I'm relieved of my duties next week?"

"I'll pay you until the end of the month. You can have a few extra days to plan your trip." I offered with a smile.

That worked. She beamed at me. "You have been a most generous, kind employer, Mr. Grayson. I'm sure the next woman will think so as well. Such a gentleman. So thoughtful."

I glanced at my watch, trying not to laugh. I doubted the man I'd shot through the head last week would consider me kind and thoughtful.

She had no idea. Neither did any of her predecessors. I planned to keep it that way with Taliyah.

"I have a meeting. I'll be gone most of the day."

"Oh, a new client?"

"Yes," I lied smoothly.

"Wonderful. I'll lock up when I leave."

"You do that."

I headed to my office and grabbed my props. My briefcase, coat, and cell phone. I checked that everything was locked and in place. The chances of Joyce even coming into my office were slim. She knew I was intensely private and preferred my office not be entered if I wasn't there, but on occasion, she left mail or things for me to sign on my desk. She never touched anything or appeared to be even curious, so I trusted her.

I hoped the same would hold true for her successor.

I waved as I left, heading for the stairs at the end of the long hallway. Or at least Joyce thought I was. Instead, I stopped at the locked doorway marked Utilities. I pressed my thumb into the hidden scanner. The door beside the large closet opened silently, and I slipped in, shutting it behind me.

Inside, my other office waited. A huge desk, a wall of monitors, and a large table where I met with my men of Hidden Justice, as we'd been named, took up most of the space. My desk held three more computers, all run from the office in the basement. A server room, second to none, was housed there and run by Damien, one of Marcus's old team members. The building was constantly monitored. Every business inside the building was part of the agency. On the second floor was the counseling office, the doctor's office beside it, both taking up the majority of the space. The top floor was where I ran the security company.

The main floor was rented out to two commercial businesses that had access from the outside. One was a small café, the other a convenience store. Both prospered here, the café busy all day with customers from the businesses both in the building and others surrounding it. The convenience store came in handy and did well in the evenings for last-minute items. I kept their rent low to keep them open. There was a small area on the main floor where packages were dropped off, other items delivered, maintenance men signed in and escorted to the right areas. No one outside the organization was allowed to roam the building unescorted. The men who staffed the front desk were all older ex-agents. I paid them well and kept them happy. In turn, they kept the building safe. The one exception to it all was Leo. He had been one of Marcus's men and had been badly injured in a situation gone awry. He was listed as the building's manager, and he worked with Damien a lot of the time. He had a private office on the main floor, and he kept the building going, helped us when required behind the scenes, and never had to pick up a gun again. He was a favorite with the tenants and had come a long way from the beaten, broken shell of a man left to die on the floor. His wife and baby helped, and secure employment gave him focus.

I had bought the building years ago and built it around the agency. When Marcus left the organization and his team disbanded, I brought Damien on board and switched roles. I no longer oversaw only one team. Instead, I looked after several smaller ones. I was like the chess master, moving pieces around as needed. Various teams going various places all over the country. I worked with all their leaders, assigning roles and operations best suited to the team they ran. And there were times I stepped in and was part of the team. I needed that connection, and I had to admit, I still craved the edge of danger it came with.

I saw a need for some of the agents who stepped away from the game early. Those who still had a lot to offer, but not on the level we dealt with. For some recruits who realized they didn't want the constant stress and emotional duress of what Hidden Justice constantly did to a psyche. I formed Elite Security, and we kept the agents in-house and employed. We catered to high-end clients and events. The people we protected had no idea that the men guarding them had training so lethal, they could clear a room in seconds without much effort. Luckily nothing even remotely close to that happened. The occasional overzealous fan of visiting celebrities, pushy entrepreneurs wanting to talk to local businessmen about their ideas, or a wedding crasher for society's elite were about the highest danger we ran into. Among our biggest clients were the men of BAM, who hired us to oversee their charity events. Aiden Callaghan had used us for various gigs once he'd decided to step back as he grew close to retirement. We had a good working relationship. Aiden had confided in me about the events that had led to Bentley's wife being kidnapped and his never-ending worry that something would happen to her again. I had assured him it never would on our watch. He thought I was joking when I informed him trained killers would be on alert every moment we were under contract with them.

I wasn't.

Bentley would never have to be concerned over his wife's safety. Or anyone else at BAM we were hired to protect.

I was the owner/manager of the business. The front man. It was a good cover, and I stayed close to the shadows while still maintaining a presence. No one ever suspected what I really did, and I made sure to keep it that way. None of the ex-agents I used were linked in any way to Hidden Justice, and we stayed under the radar. It was a win-win situation all around. I kept my hand in Hidden Justice and employed the agents who deserved the chance. The life demanded by this calling was not for everyone.

And I did it all from a secret office hidden in plain sight behind the one visible to the public. I had discovered early on in my career that people tended to overlook what was right in front of them if distracted by something else. Like a magician relying on sleight of hand to have you look elsewhere so he could pull off an illusion so breathtakingly real you never thought to question it.

I sat down, checking the cameras. Joyce was at her desk, afghan on the go. My office was empty. Damien was busy on his various laptops and computers downstairs, waving when he saw me signed in. I knew he'd be up soon to discuss the next case or client.

Meanwhile, I used our servers to find out what I could about the beautiful woman I had stupidly hired.

I needed to be fully armed with information in order to prepare myself.

I ignored the laughter in my head that informed me you could never fully prepare for a hurricane.

I found nothing suspicious about Taliyah Wells. Her age and birth date checked out. She was born in Alberta but moved to Quebec when she was young. Parents were deceased. She was raised by her grandmother, whom I could find little on except the basics, which wasn't surprising. Her life had been lived before the invention of the internet. She had a sibling, but he was deceased as well, so she was alone in the world.

Taliyah had a high grade point average, thousands of dollars in outstanding student loans as she claimed, and lived in a basement apartment off Dundas Street. I hacked in to the employment records of 7&7. She'd worked there for six months, clean record, and her employee file had little in it to help me in any way.

I noted a lack of information for a two-year stretch, which was curious, but when I backtracked, I realized she had lost her grandmother and brother close together around the beginning of that time frame, so it could be explained easily with taking time off to grieve. She didn't attend school or work in that missing expanse, which explained her later-in-life graduation from university.

I found pictures from some social media sites from her younger days before she'd lost her brother and grandmother. Interestingly enough, she had no Facebook, Instagram, or any other account anymore. The older pictures showed a youthful but still beautiful version of her. She was serious-looking in most pictures, much as she had been while sitting across from me. I had a feeling that smiles were rare for her. I had to wonder how she functioned as a bartender. Was she aloof and mysterious? Friendly but quiet?

I might have to find out for myself. Just to understand her, of course.

I clicked off, glancing at the security screens. Joyce was at her desk, her head bowed, fingers busy with her knitting. The halls were empty, the café busy, and all was well. Everything ran with a smooth efficiency that pleased me.

Damien came in, coffees in hand and a laptop tucked under his arm.

"Hey, Julian."

I accept a cup gratefully. One thing Joyce did badly was make coffee. It was akin to drinking dark water. We kept the café downstairs busy every day with coffee orders.

"Find a new Joyce?"

I sipped the black brew, giving myself a moment before I answered. "Yeah."

"When does she start?"

"Monday."

"I don't suppose you hired someone who bakes this time? Makes good coffee?"

"Strangely enough, those questions didn't come up during the interview," I stated dryly.

"They should. I don't need another afghan."

I chuckled. "I doubt Taliyah knits afghans."

He lifted his eyebrows. "Taliyah?"

"That's her name." I pushed her résumé toward him. "She's younger than the usual Joyce."

He read the document, pursing his lips in surprise. "Definitely not another Joyce."

I shrugged. "Time for a change."

He nodded slowly. "Right."

"I got the feeling she was pretty desperate."

"Need me to check her out?"

"I did. She's clean. I don't think her art history degree is going to pay the bills, though."

"Oh yeah. Those jobs are hard to come by."

"She's got spunk. She convinced the agency to send her."

"And she convinced you to hire her," he added.

"I can always revoke that if she doesn't work out. I gave her a one-month trial."

He studied me but didn't say anything.

I met his gaze steadily. "You got anything on that situation in Ottawa?"

He handed me a file. "Yeah. I think we have all the pieces."

"Great. Let's get it going."

Monday, I waited eagerly for Taliyah to arrive. She was early, garbed in another pretty dress that showed off her legs. She had her hair pulled up and back, tiny bunches of curls escaping from her attempt to tame them and showing off the elegant line of her neck.

She sat with Joyce, listening, taking notes, and asking questions. I kept my door open at times, and others, I watched from the hidden cameras. She was a delight to study, her expressions open and honest. She would make a horrible poker player. I'd already discovered when she was unsure, she nibbled on her bottom lip. When confused, she tugged on her ear. When she understood something, the right side of her mouth curled into a brief crooked grin and she tapped her chin with the pen or pencil she was holding. She had an unconscious way of smoothing back her hair from her head, which did little good. Corkscrew curls returned to the spot she cleared almost instantly. I tried not to be envious of those curls touching her head and neck.

With a groan, I stood and paced my office. This had to stop.

The security guys showed up as they always did after a weekend, filling in reports, time cards, collecting their next assignments. I always spoke with them personally, making sure everything was all right. Everyone had something to say about Taliyah, and I made it plain there was no office fraternization allowed, as per my rules. To their credit, not one of them reminded me there had never been a rule like that until today.

Luckily, most of them seemed more curious than anything, so I was able to relax.

Around eleven, there was a knock at my door, and Taliyah came in after I called out for her to enter. She approached my desk, carrying a cup of coffee and the mail.

I eyed the cup with speculation and accepted the mail.

"Finding everything all right?" I asked as if I hadn't been glued to my screen watching her. I indicated the chair in front of my desk and was treated to the sight of her long legs being crossed again.

"Oh yes," she assured me. "Joyce is a very good teacher. I've used the program she has before, so I understand it." She bit her lip. "I think it could be used a little more productively," she added in a whisper.

I tried not to laugh. I waved my hand in the

direction of the front office. "Feel free. Once she leaves, make it yours."

"I made the coffee," she said. "Joyce said she used four scoops. I used seven." She pulled a face. "Otherwise, why bother? It's just hot water with some color."

Once again, I was amused, but I lifted my cup and took a sip. It was way better than Joyce's had ever been.

"I'll keep it our secret."

"Thanks."

I cleared my throat, shoving down the temptation to simply talk to her. I needed to act like a professional.

"My office is private," I began. "When I'm not here, no one is allowed in."

She nodded, not saying anything.

"I'm out at meetings a lot. Looking for new business, meeting with current clients." I lied smoothly. "I often come and go using my private entrance." I indicated the door that led to the hall. "If I'm not here and anyone knocks on that door, do not open it. Do you understand?"

Her eyes went round, a trace of fear in them.

"It's simply a precaution. No one should be in the building unless they are supposed to be here."

"Yes, I saw the security desk when I arrived last week and was signed in. I met Leo this morning, and he gave me my pass and explained how to use it."

"Good."

"So, you'll leave, and I won't know you're gone?" she asked.

"No, I'll always let you know, but I often slip out that way. I like to use the stairs, and it's closer."

"Ah, a fitness guy. I thought you worked out, given your, ah…" She trailed off, not finishing her sentence.

"My, ah…?" I had to ask her.

Color diffused along the tops of her cheekbones, and since her hair was pulled back, I noticed the tops of her ears also darkened. It was rather…endearing.

"You obviously keep in shape," she murmured.

I let her off the hook. "I try."

"Okay, so your office is private, you're out a lot, I answer the phones, field general inquiries, send all serious ones to you, schedule the guys for jobs, follow up with time cards, and do the payroll entry, plus knit afghans?" She wrinkled her nose. "I'm not sure about the last one, but the rest I can handle."

I chuckled at her drollness. "There is a lot of quiet time. Joyce fills hers in with knitting."

"Could I do schoolwork?"

"I thought you graduated?"

"I have. But I want my master's. So, I want to keep taking courses, and some I can do online."

"Then, yes, when it's quiet, I have no objection." I drained my coffee. "As long as your work is done, then it's fine."

"I'll always get my work done." She stood. "I'll go and sit with Joyce again."

I thanked her for the coffee and tried not to notice how her hips swayed as she walked out. The way the hem of her dress brushed the backs of her knees. I was almost grateful when she shut the door behind her.

Almost.

I shut my eyes and shook my head. I needed to get a grip.

She was my secretary.

That was all.

———

By the end of Tuesday, Joyce came to me. "I have shown Taliyah everything. She's picked it up quickly. I don't think you or she need me anymore."

"So, you're done with me?" I teased her.

"I think it's the other way around, Mr. Grayson."

I rounded the desk and handed her a flat box. "Many thanks for your work, Joyce. I will miss you."

A sly smile lit her face. "Not so much, I think, with her out front."

I ignored her subtle teasing. "The clicking of your knitting needles was very soothing."

She chuckled and patted my arm in a maternal gesture. "It's been a pleasure, Mr. Grayson. Thank you for your indulgence."

I indicated the box. "Thank you."

I knew she would love it. I had bought her a gift certificate at her favorite wool shop. Taliyah had found out the name for me and had, in fact, purchased and wrapped it with the travel voucher I'd bought for Joyce as well from all the staff. Everyone had liked Joyce.

She tapped the box, her eyes surprisingly damp. "I appreciate it. Now be good to that young lady out there."

"Am I that much of an ogre you have to warn me?"

She paused before leaving. "I think her reach will go far beyond that desk."

Then with those cryptic words, she left.

For the next couple of weeks, we fell into a pattern. Taliyah was there early every day. She worked hard, made a great cup of coffee, and for the most part, ignored me. I was fascinated watching her. She changed something every day. She adjusted her desk, rearranged the chairs in the outer office. Moved the few pictures that hung on the walls. Brought in flowers for her desk to brighten the area. She liked to stay busy.

No matter what I was doing, what office I was in, I was drawn to the monitor that showed me her. She spent six full days rearranging the file cabinet. Sorting, organizing, stapling until she seemed satisfied. The outer office was immaculate—she seemed to stay busy every moment. She was professional and friendly to the guys, although I noticed her real smiles were still rare. It was as if she carried something heavy and sad with her.

I tried to fight the desire to know what that was and erase it.

She was polite and distant with me. She brought me coffee every day, answered my questions without saying a thing or giving me a clue as to what was going on behind those beautiful eyes. We had very little personal interaction, which was exactly what I wanted in my secretary.

Except I hated it.

I wanted to know what she was thinking, feeling, wondering. What drove her to want this dead-end job when she could be doing something far more suited to her talents. She'd be an excellent PA for some bigwig executive or run an entire office with ease, instead of being here.

But selfishly, I kept my mouth shut.

Because I wanted her here.

I sat behind my desk in my hidden office, going over the intel on a new assignment. I picked the team that would suit the operation the best and planned on meeting with them later today in another location. I never brought them here together.

Movement caught my eye on the monitor beside me, and I looked up, startled to see the light on in my office. I frowned as I watched Taliyah enter, pausing in the doorway, looking around in curiosity. My hand tightened on the pen I was gripping.

Why was she in my office? She had never entered it while I was out before now. She knew my feelings on it.

I relaxed when I saw the package tucked under her arm and some envelopes in her hand. She was just putting the mail on my desk.

Except, after she set it down, she paused, and I watched as she sat down in my chair, her gaze focused on the left-hand side of my desk. I zoomed in to the stack of files and papers sitting there. There were contracts, notes, files for Elite Security—nothing of great interest.

What had caught her attention?

She nibbled on her bottom lip. Tugged on her ear. Smoothed back her hair.

My suspicion grew. She was nervous. She knew she shouldn't be in my office.

What was she after? Was she more than I thought? A plant? Did someone suspect something? Anger churned in my stomach. Had I been so blind to her beauty, I had missed all the signs?

She stood, bending over my desk, and her hands began to move quickly. Her hair fell forward, obscuring her actions. I couldn't get the camera angle positioned correctly to see exactly what she was doing. She stayed busy for about five minutes then stood back, nodded, and tapped her chin. She pushed my chair back in place, reached over and fiddled with something else, then hurried out of my office. At her desk, she grabbed her purse and left, hanging the unneeded little sign Joyce always used when she left for lunch stating the office was closed. I followed her flight out of the building right to the café.

I stood and slipped into my other office through the hidden panel behind my desk. Damien and I had installed it, and it was a useful feature at times such as this. I stared at the surface of my desk, finally comprehending what she had done. She hadn't touched a drawer or searched for anything. But she *had* been busy.

The haphazard pile of files was straight and

uniform. Color coded, even, from lightest to darkest. The papers were tucked into the correct files. My pens were in the holder, all nib side down. My stapler and Post-it notes were lined up with precision. My lamp at a precise forty-five-degree angle.

A smile tugged on my lips. Taliyah was a neat freak. She liked things in their place. I had noticed her way of straightening out the coffee cup handles so they aligned. The perfectly legible and precise new labels on the files. The new file folders themselves. It explained the rearranging of the office. The pictures.

And now my desk. She couldn't help herself.

Relief tore through me when I realized how crazy my impulse had been that she was after something. My gut told me she wasn't anything other than what she seemed.

An efficient, beautiful distraction.

Just for fun, I decided to play a trick on her.

I wanted to see her reaction.

I was hoping to be rewarded with a smile.

Later that afternoon, I strolled by her desk, trying not to smirk. "Any coffee?"

"Of course."

"Great."

In my office, I sat down, pushing the file folders askew, then I picked up a pen and opened one of the files. She entered and set down the steaming cup. I indicated the chair, watching her as she sat and crossed her legs. Today's dress had a slit in the front that offered me a great view of those sexy calves. I watched her reaction as she looked over my desk, her teeth instantly finding her bottom lip.

"Something wrong?" I asked.

"No."

I nodded slowly. "Everything going well? You settled in and finding everything you need?" I closed the file, leaving a paper on the top, and tossed it carelessly to the side. Her eyes tracked my movement. She smoothed her hair back.

I tried not to laugh.

"Yes," she replied.

I tapped the pen on my chin, then pitched it into the holder, nib side up. I picked up a Post-it note and grabbed another pen, unscrewing the cap and jotting down a number. I frowned, crumpled it, and threw it heedlessly, taking another one and knocking over the pile. I rewrote the number, dropped the pen to the desk and ignored the cap, handing her the Post-it.

"I like pizza from this place. Can you call and order a large 'all in' one for delivery?"

She took the paper, her eyes on my desk. "Of course."

"Ask for Carlos. Tell him it's for me. He knows. He keeps my credit card on file."

She nodded, her gaze bouncing from one untidy mess to another. I searched through the files, spreading them like a deck of cards and picking one, leaving the rest alone. I opened it, shoving some of the papers by my elbow.

That broke her.

She stood. "Are you going out of the office again today?" she asked, her voice actually squeaking on the last word.

"No." I smirked at her. "In all afternoon. I have a couple of phone meetings. If you'd order the pizza, that would be great." I stood and walked over the fridge and bent to get a bottle of water, waiting to see what she would do.

She didn't disappoint.

In a second, she had rounded the desk, straightening the files and capping the pen, upending the one in the holder so it was pointing in the correct direction. She tapped the Post-its into place and moved the stapler a fraction. She tossed the crumpled Post-it in the garbage. Then she huffed and lifted her gaze to mine.

I winked at her.

"You did that deliberately!"

"I noticed the precise piles when I got back into my office. I wanted to see if there was a fairy in here or my secretary."

"I had mail," she protested. "And it was a mess. I just organized it. You can work more efficiently when organized. I didn't snoop or do anything."

"You are very proficient."

"You're an ass."

My eyebrows flew up, and a bark of laughter escaped my lips at her unexpected term. "What did you call me?"

"You heard me. An ass." She waved her hand

toward my desk. "I like order. It calms me. You didn't have to make fun of me."

She stalked past me, and, without thinking, I reached out, holding her arm and halting her progress.

"Hey, Tally, I'm sorry. I didn't mean to offend you. I was teasing."

"What did you call me?" She threw back my earlier question.

"Ah, Tally. Sorry if that offends too."

"My gran used to call me that."

"And that brings up painful memories?" I asked quietly, stepping closer.

"No," she whispered.

"I noticed how tidy my desk was. I thought…well, frankly, I thought it was adorable. I figured out mess drives you crazy. I was trying to see how far I could push you before you broke." I smiled as I tucked a loose piece of hair behind her ear. "It didn't take much."

"You found it *adorable*?"

"Yes."

"I shouldn't have called you an ass."

I leaned closer. "To be honest, I found that adorable too."

The smile I had been hoping for broke through, lifting the corners of her mouth and crinkling her lovely eyes. "Really?"

With a start, I realized how close we were standing. The fact that I still had a curl wrapped around my finger. How incredibly enticing she smelled. Like warm honey and citrus. The frightening part was that I wanted to be even closer. I wanted to pull her against me and inhale her into my lungs. Meld her close to my body. Taste her.

Instead, I released the curl and stepped back. "Really. But I didn't mean to offend."

"You didn't. Honest. I was just shocked you noticed. Most people don't." She cocked her head to the side, a small smile still playing on her lips. "I guess that's part of the job, right? Noticing details others wouldn't."

"Pardon?"

"The security thing."

"Oh, yes. Part of it, for sure."

I took another step back, hating the distance between us. "I apologize for overstepping."

For a moment, she said nothing. Then once again, she smiled. "I guess you owe me pizza, then, Commander."

Her use of the term commander threw me for a moment, then I smiled. She had heard the guys refer to me that way—old habits from their days at Hidden Justice. They liked to use the term, and I had stopped objecting.

"I guess so, Taliyah."

"Tally. You can call me Tally if you want."

"Okay."

"Can I call you Jules? Or maybe Juju?" She clapped her hands. "Maybe Jujube."

"*No.*"

She burst out laughing, the sound melodic and light. "You should see the look on your face. I was kidding. But I'm getting an extra-large pizza."

"Fine," I grumped, fighting back my smile.

"And keep your desk neat. I can't stop myself at times," she threw over her shoulder as she walked out of the office.

I chuckled and headed to my desk. Two smiles, a laugh, teasing, a late lunch sharing my favorite pizza, and a nickname. And I'd touched her hair.

Look how far we'd come in an afternoon.

I was doing well with ignoring the pretty woman I'd hired to be my secretary.

I ignored the mocking laughter in my head.

CHAPTER THREE

Tally

I couldn't believe I was sitting across from my new boss eating pizza.

I couldn't believe I'd called him an ass.

And I really couldn't believe he'd laughed. Or that he found me adorable.

I had no idea why I got so upset. Except it meant he saw—he noticed. I tried not to get noticed anymore.

And his reaction…his words, the way he touched my hair and called me Tally. He was honestly taken aback by my anger.

When he stepped closer, into my space, I should have been screaming for him to back off—except I *wanted* him closer. I wanted to feel his warmth, smell his rich, aromatic scent. Crisp fall air and spice. It was clean, heady, and suited him.

The moment I met him, he overwhelmed me. When I had heard one of the other women who was interviewed earlier in the day complain the building was like Fort Knox to get into and say she refused to work somewhere with so many security restrictions, I had begged the agent to give me the information. She had shaken her head.

"They prefer, ah, a more mature woman, dear. It's a bit of a dull job. It's not for you."

"Please, I want to try."

She pursed her lips. "Interviews are over in forty-five minutes. He only ever interviews for one day."

"I can make it."

I had hopped the subway to the closest station and run the rest of the way, barely making it.

Mr. Grayson hadn't been what I expected. Far younger, handsomer, and tall. His shoulders were broad, his arms thick, the muscles rippling as he moved. His dark brown hair was long, wavy, and messy, as if he spent a lot of time running his hands through it. His beard was short and neat, setting off his full lips and framing his chiseled jawline. And his eyes. Warm hazel —bright brown and green, with gold flecks so large they were like bursts of fire around his pupils—and set under heavy, straight eyebrows that emphasized their uniqueness. They were mesmerizing. He moved with the confidence of a man who was used to being in control. He had seemed as determined as the agency that this job wasn't for me, but the thought of being in that building, safe and protected four days a week, was too much to resist. I had somehow gotten the job, determined to be the best secretary he'd ever had.

Convinced I could ignore the attraction I felt toward him.

"Tally? What's wrong?"

Julian's low, concerned voice brought me out of my musings. His focused gaze met mine, and I shook my head to clear it.

"Nothing. I was just thinking this is the best pizza I have ever eaten."

"You've been thinking about it for five minutes. I wondered if the pepperoni wasn't uniformly distributed on the pizza and you were reconfiguring it in your head." He lifted one eyebrow, the quizzical look on his face comical. "Or am I being an ass again?"

I had to laugh. "No. Very funny. That doesn't bother me. The space around me does."

"I get that. Damien is like that."

"The IT guy I met the other day?"

His lips quirked. "Yep. The IT guy."

"I guess you'd have to be, with all that entails."

He nodded, chewing and swallowing. He ate slowly, enjoying his food. He was relaxed, sitting at his desk, his tie loose and his sleeves rolled up. His forearms rippled as he lifted the pizza to his mouth, and I noticed the light dusting of dark hair on them. I was certain I saw a hint of ink peeking out on occasion, which made me curious.

"So, are you part of the team?" I asked.

His head snapped up. "What?"

I frowned, wondering what I'd said that made him respond that way. "One of the people who works the security jobs."

"Oh." He visibly relaxed. "No. Not anymore anyway. Now, I just oversee. Bring in new business."

"But you did?"

He bit into his pizza, chewing and looking thoughtful. "I was more actively involved than I am now."

"Oh?" I asked, wondering if he would share at all.

"I was shot. It curtailed my effectiveness somewhat."

I dropped my pizza and stared at him in horror. "You were shot?"

He nodded with a frown. "No need to look so upset, Tally. I'm alive and well. I changed direction in my life, though."

"I'm sorry. It's just that I hate violence."

He lifted his eyebrows. "I see."

"Where?" I asked before I could stop myself.

"Shoulder and both knees. It was in my old line of work, not with Elite Security."

"When you were a cop," I murmured, remembering I had read that in his bio.

He looked away but nodded, and I realized he didn't want to discuss it.

There was quiet for a moment, then he spoke.

"So, an art major. What do you see yourself doing with that?"

I snorted. "Not much, apparently."

He chuckled. "No, really, what did you have in mind?"

I set down my pizza, wiping my fingers. "I have always loved art. Painting, sculptures, drawings. Anything visual. Even the art of music or poetry. I love the beauty of brushstrokes on a canvas. How clay can be molded. Marble chiseled. It speaks to my soul."

"Do you do any of that?" he asked quietly.

"I paint and draw."

"Are you any good?"

"Not good enough to make a living, but good enough to do it," I responded. "I specialized in art history. I wanted to get hired at a museum or a gallery. Learn. Become a curator. Discover new artists. Show the world the old masters. But it takes time and connections. Right now, I would be happy to be a volunteer and get my foot in the door. And I have to do my master's, which is more schooling."

"And you bartend? Do you enjoy it?"

"Not really. But it pays well, the hours are steady, and I'm behind the bar. I tried waitressing—not my thing. It's only two nights a week, but it brings in a good income."

"Rough crowd there?"

"On occasion. But we're pretty small, so it's mostly regulars. Sometimes if an event is in town, we're close enough to the main drag to get the overflow and it can get out of hand, but we have security at the door."

He studied me, then leaned forward. "If you're ever worried or fearful, you call me. All right, Tally? It doesn't matter what time it is. Promise me."

"Call you?" I repeated. "For what?"

"I'll come and get you. Take you anywhere you need to be. Make sure you're safe."

His statement left me stunned. He was serious.

Make sure you're safe. He had no idea what that meant to me.

Unbidden, tears sprang to my eyes, and I had to get

out of there before he saw how emotional his words made me.

"Thanks, Julian. I'll remember that." I stood. "And thanks for the pizza. I appreciate it."

"Where are you going?" he asked.

"Back to work," I said brightly. "I've slacked off enough, and I want to finish a couple more additions to the schedule before I go."

"Tally—"

I cut him off.

"Make sure to tidy your desk before you leave, or I'll think about it all weekend," I teased, not wanting him to push the subject.

He took the hint the way I had done earlier.

"Okay. I'll line it all up before I go."

I felt his stare all the way back to my desk, even with his door closed.

I sat down heavily. I hadn't expected to feel this allure to my boss. To hear those words from his lips and want to throw my arms around his neck and let him hold me. To tell him how safe I felt just being in the same office as he was. I hadn't planned on the desire that hummed through my veins every time he was close. I couldn't let him get close.

I couldn't put him in danger. I already cared too much.

JULIAN

I looked forward to Monday morning far too much. Even though Tally wasn't supposed to start until ten, I knew she would be at her desk before nine. Often, I was in my secret office, watching as she came in, settling at her desk, making coffee, checking voice mail, and getting ready for the day. I enjoyed the chance to study her, watching the way her brow furrowed as she scribbled messages or reread something on her laptop. Today, she wore her hair down, the curls cascading over her shoulders, the color bright under the lights. It sometimes appeared to annoy her, but I loved the curls and often had to refrain from touching them if she was close.

It occurred to me that the weekends seemed endless now. The office dimmed a little when she left, and I found myself thinking of her a lot. I knew I needed to stop. Stop thinking, stop watching, stop finding excuses to go to her desk or call her into my office so I could be close to her. To hear her voice, be rewarded with one of her rare smiles.

The more I studied her, the more I realized that there was always something lurking behind her eyes— something profoundly sad, something that called to me. Yet I had no idea what it was or why she affected me the way she did. There was also a lingering feeling of fear she tried to cover. I sensed it in her the first day she came into the office, and it often manifested itself without her realizing. She shrank a little when a new face appeared, a sudden noise made her jump, she seemed to linger when it was time to leave. Even though no one would come into the office without her knowing, she locked the door when I left, only disengaging it when she expected me back. Something, someone, had placed that fear inside her.

I wanted to erase that residual sadness and eradicate her fear. But it wasn't my place.

I watched her for a few more moments, then turned my head and rubbed my eyes. I was becoming a stalker, observing and watching her constantly. I needed to stop my behavior. I stood, grimacing a little. The mission I had been part of on the weekend had been taxing. I had taken a few well-aimed punches to the ribs before I was able to subdue the man I had been chasing. Once we had extracted the information we needed, my bullet paid him back for the pain. I took great delight in destroying the child porn ring he had been part of. None of the group saw dawn, and their filth was wiped out. We found several promising leads to other groups, and Damien had been busy with the intel. By tonight, many of them would be up in flames. By tomorrow, all of them gone.

I glanced back at the screen, pausing. Tally stared out the window, a wistful look on her face, and I wondered what she was thinking. What did she long for out there that caused her such sadness?

I switched off the monitor. Once again, I reminded myself it wasn't my business.

I wasn't in the position to be anything other than a boss to her. She was young, still looking for her life, and already fearful. The only thing I could offer her was a tenuous, complicated relationship, more fear, and the repercussions of being involved with me. It was too dangerous. Her words, "I hate violence," said it all.

The arguing voice in my head told me that no one could protect her better than I could. That with me in her life, her fear could be eased. The sadness drained from her eyes.

I had to ignore that voice.

It was nothing but a hopeful lie.

———

For the next two weeks, I managed to be exactly what I had set out to be—Taliyah's boss. I was courteous, respectful, and distant. The way I had been with every one of the women who had come before her. I forced myself not to go to her desk. I got my own coffee. I used the intercom and kept my door shut. Distance was what I needed to get over this little fascination with her. That was all, I convinced myself. If she noticed anything different, she never said a word. She did her job efficiently, and when she wasn't busy for me, she worked on some online course she was taking. I resisted mirroring her screen to see what it was about. I found it more difficult than I expected. Somehow, simply being close to her seemed to bring me a calm I had never experienced. Gaining a rare smile from her made my chest warm. I found I hated Wednesdays—the one day she wasn't in the office. Even with my limited contact with her, the place seemed emptier and incomplete without her around. I wondered how long I could keep up feigning indifference.

There was a knock at my door Thursday morning, and I called out for her to enter. She stepped in, looking hesitant.

"Yes, Taliyah?"

"Ah, my boss at 7&7 just called and asked if I could cover tonight and the afternoon shift tomorrow. One of the other bartenders just quit."

"I see."

"I can come in for the morning tomorrow and make up the other hours next week. I'm caught up on the schedule, and payroll isn't until Monday."

"Sure, that's fine. So, you're leaving early?" I asked, tamping down my disappointment.

"Just an hour or so. I need to go home and get my uniform."

"Right. That's fine," I assured her. "I have an outside meeting in the morning, so I will see you Monday." I glanced at my watch. "In fact, I have one shortly, so I'll say goodbye now, and I'll head out soon. Be sure to lock the place up when you leave."

She paused as if she was about to say something, then changed her mind.

"Have a good weekend, Julian."

I smiled benignly. "You as well."

She left, shutting the door behind her. I gathered my things and, keeping up the charade, used the door to the hall, shutting it loudly so she would hear it, and heading to the other doorway, slipping inside the Hidden Justice room. Damien was already waiting, full of information.

Grateful for the distraction, I pushed aside all other thoughts and got down to business.

Late Friday night, I stepped from my car, my head filled with the images I had seen. The sights and smells of those raids never got easier. They wore on a man, and tonight, I was feeling it all the way down into my bones. Marcus and Matteo had been right when they stepped away, citing the fact that this was a never-ending job. For every horror show we shut down, another sprang up. I had never been out in the field the way they were. My old injuries precluded me from being effective that way, but the last while, I had joined in more raids, and it was draining me. The darkness swirled around in my brain, and I didn't seem to be able to turn it off. I felt a disconnect, a sadness I couldn't manage to shake.

I paused on the way to the elevator. Upstairs, my apartment was empty. Dark. The refrigerator no doubt containing whatever leftovers I had shoved in it last week, probably no longer palatable. It wasn't food I wanted so much as some human contact. Something that would connect me back to this world. I turned and headed up the ramp and onto the street. Before I even realized where I was going, I was in front of 7&7. I peered inside the bar, noting it was busy but not crazy. I pulled open the door and headed straight to the bar, taking a seat on the end.

I scanned the area with a frown. Taliyah wasn't anywhere to be seen. Just as I was about to ask another bartender, she came through the swinging door, plates in her hands. I watched as she slid them in front of a couple of patrons, then poured fresh beers for them. She was polite and smiling, although I was certain it was more of an act than real. She wiped the counter while talking to the customers, and I studied her.

Her hair was piled on her head, the curls still escaping in corkscrews over her shoulders. The "uniform" she wore consisted of a tight, logo-emblazed green T-shirt and a pair of black shorts. She wore an apron cinched at the waist, and she had a towel thrown over her shoulder. When she bent to pick up something, I had an unobstructed view of her curvy ass and the backs of her luscious legs. The thought of anyone else seeing them didn't sit well with me, and I made a noise in the back of my throat. The man next to me glanced my way, picked up his beer, and moved.

Taliyah looked across the bar, her eyes growing round when she met my stare. She picked up a menu and headed toward me, a bemused smile on her face.

"Julian," she greeted me.

"Taliyah."

"What are you doing here? It's late."

"I needed a drink."

"And you happened to stumble into the bar I worked at?" she teased.

"Of all the gin joints…" I trailed off with a teasing grin. Then I shrugged.

"I live around the block. It was convenient."

Three blocks, but whatever. Close enough.

"What can I get you?"

"Double scotch. Neat."

She nodded, sliding a glass in front of me and pouring in the amber liquid.

I lifted it, tilting the glass in her direction.

"To forgetting."

I downed it in one long swallow.

I tapped the bar, already feeling the warmth of the liquor curling around my chest.

"Hit me again."

She frowned and filled my glass. I picked it up and sipped this time, but the glass was empty by the time she filled a few drink orders and came back to check on me. The alcohol had softened the painful edges of my mind, and I smirked at her.

"Hi. More please."

"You need to eat something."

"You're not my mother, Tally."

"Oh, now I'm Tally again?"

I crooked my finger, and she leaned over the bar, meeting me partway.

"You're always Tally in my head when I think of you."

"And you do that a lot, do you?"

I tapped my forehead. "In here."

"Have you eaten today?"

"Momma Tally. I'll make you a deal. Bring me something to eat and another double scotch."

"I should cut you off is what I should do."

I waved my hand. "Later. You can cut me off and pour me into a cab."

"I'm getting you food."

"And scotch," I called out, watching her walk away, the shorts clinging to her like a second skin.

I hated that other men could see what I was looking at, but I had to admit, I was enjoying the view.

So I kept watching.

CHAPTER FOUR
Julian

T ally slid a plate in front of me, along with a glass of water and a shot of scotch.

"I like doubles."

"You get a single until you've eaten."

Earlier, the thought of food made my stomach clench, but now that I smelled the cheeseburger in front of me, I was starving.

The words were out before I could stop them. "You get a break?"

"In about fifteen minutes."

"Join me."

She frowned. "I'm not sure—"

I cut her off. "It wasn't an invitation."

She narrowed her eyes, studying me. Then she shook her head. "Fine. Eat."

I attacked the burger, the hot meat and melted cheese greasy and perfect. I ate the fries, adding lots of ketchup to them. I drank the water, feeling some of the despair and lethargy lifting. I also downed the scotch, plus got the other bartender to hit me with another double. When Tally sat down next to me with a cup of coffee, I smiled.

"See, I can be good, Momma T."

She laughed. "How are you feeling?"

"Better." I picked up my scotch. "Much better."

She looked at the glass with a frown, figuring out I'd snuck more scotch.

"What happened, Julian?"

I could never tell her. Never say the words to describe the horrors and atrocities I saw all the time. Although Evie knew what he did, Matteo had shielded her from it, and Marcus had tried to do the same with Missy, although she had already been involved. But Tally was different. She was completely unaware of what I did —of the secret organization I was part of. What we did to try to clean up the world of the evil that lurked below the façade of everyday life.

"Just a bad day." Then I smiled, still drunk enough to say stupid shit. "I missed you in the office today. No one straightened my files or made me a cup of coffee."

"I see."

"And I didn't get my smile."

"What?"

"Every day. I try to get you to smile every day. It's like a little bonus."

"You're not making any sense, Julian."

I turned and faced her fully, our knees pressed together. I could feel the warmth of her skin through the material of my pants. I wanted to touch her to see if it was as soft as I thought it would be, but I refrained. "You always look sad. I like it when you smile. I like it when I make you smile. Really smile. Not like the fake ones you have to put on here or when you say hi to the guys."

"There's a difference?" she asked quietly.

"Yes. Your eyes change. Such beautiful eyes," I murmured. "So mesmerizing."

She blinked and slid off the stool. "I have to get back."

"Already?"

"I have to use the restroom. I only get a short break."

She hurried away, and I signaled the other bartender for another scotch, determined to sip this one slowly. Unlike Tally, she didn't care how many I'd had and filled my glass.

Tally returned, frowning at me again. "*No* more scotch, Julian."

I waved my finger. "You're not smiling."

"I'm getting you coffee."

The other bartender came over and said something to Tally. She glanced my way and leaned close. "I have to help in the kitchen. Stop drinking, Julian. Please."

I nodded. "Coffee."

"Yes." She poured me a cup and slid it my way. "Behave."

She disappeared, and suddenly, it all came back. The images, the horrible building we raided. The scared teenagers who should have been out with their friends at the mall, not locked in a place where they were forced to do things no kid should ever have to do. The faces of the heartless men and women who had torn them from their lives. Lives they would be returned to, yet never be the same. I had relished watching the perpetrators die, although tonight, I hadn't pulled the trigger myself. I wasn't sure what that said about my own mind-set, but I never felt guilt when I killed the scum that committed the crimes.

And as soon as Tally was gone, it all hit me again. I lifted my hand, catching the eye of the other bartender.

"Scotch. *Now.*"

<hr />

I woke up, blinking and confused. I scanned the room, recognizing my apartment. Everything looked normal, and aside from the splitting headache, I seemed to be in one piece. I had no idea how I got home. And something was different.

It took me a moment to realize someone was in bed with me. I had been asleep on top of someone, my head resting in their lap and my arms around them tightly.

I swallowed, trying not to groan.

What had I done? Picked up some strange woman and brought her back here? Fucked her?

My stomach lurched.

I had done that in front of Tally? I couldn't hold back my groan of disgust this time.

"How's your head?" a soft voice whispered above me. A voice I recognized.

Tally was in bed with me. Tally was in my apartment, in my bed. I was asleep on top of her.

Jesus—what had I done?

"Throbbing and confused," I mumbled. I pushed myself up and, with a moan, fell back on my pillow. I looked over at her, drinking in the sight of her, half sitting, half lying in my bed. Her hair spread around my pillow like wildfire. Her blue eyes looked sleepy, and a huge part of me felt relieved when I noticed she still had on her green T-shirt and I wore the T-shirt I'd had on under my sweater last night. But how had we gotten *here*? I searched my memory, but all I got was a scotch-hazed image of Tally pulling my hand and telling me to behave.

"I'm afraid to ask," I admitted.

She pulled herself up and crossed her arms in vexation. "You disobeyed me and drank way too much scotch. I gave Lillian shit about how much she let you drink. She said you seemed fine." She snorted. "Until you tried to get off the barstool and fell face-first onto the floor."

"Oh." I vaguely recalled something about trying to stand.

"I found your keys and looked at your wallet for your address. I brought you home and only meant to make sure you got inside safely, but you refused to let me go. You kept asking me to stay. You said I made it all go away."

"Oh," I repeated. It was the truth. She made things better. Easier.

"I finally got you in here and went to get you some Tylenol and water. You kicked off your shoes and pants. You got your sweater stuck trying to pull it over your head." Her lips quirked, then she frowned again. "I helped you, and you fell into bed. I gave you the pills and tried to leave, but you grabbed my hand. Asked me to sit with you." She sighed. "You sort of curled up and put your head in my lap. I stroked your head, and you seemed to like it. It relaxed you and you fell asleep. I thought you'd move and I'd leave, but you never did. I couldn't get you to unlock your arms. I guess I fell asleep too."

"I'm sorry?" I offered. I was sorry I had gotten drunk and made an idiot of myself. I wasn't sorry about holding her all night. It was the best night's sleep I'd had in months. No nightmares or images filtering through my mind. No restlessness.

"Why did you get so drunk last night?" she asked.

"Bad day."

"Not good enough."

"That's all I can say. I'm sorry I was such a handful, but really, it's none of your concern."

She met my gaze with her own, not backing down. "*None of my concern*? You come to my bar, get drunk, and practically beg me to stay with you, and it's none of my concern? I beg to differ, Julian. It's very much my concern."

I ran a hand over my face. "Leave it, Tally. It won't happen again."

"I don't get you," she replied. "You're hot and cold. One moment, you're teasing and nice. Then you're removed and distant. Every day, you say something, do something, to make me smile, and then you disappear as if I insulted you." She shook her head. "I don't understand you, Julian."

"I don't understand myself," I muttered.

"Some days, I think you regret hiring me."

"No," I swiftly denied. "I don't. It's-it's complicated, Tally. I have to be your boss. That's it. I'm sorry for my behavior, and if it's made you question working for me, I understand. But it won't happen again."

"You won't tell me why?"

I shut my eyes, my mind once again swimming with the images and sounds of yesterday.

"I had to…help someone with a bad situation. Really bad. It bothered me more than I wanted to admit."

She was quiet for a moment, then spoke. "I'm sorry."

"I shouldn't have gone to your bar and gotten drunk. I shouldn't have made you responsible for me and my welfare. I'm sorry."

She slid from my bed, smoothing down her wrinkled shirt. "I would rather you did that than go somewhere else where you may have been in danger. The city isn't a safe place, Julian."

It was all I could do not to laugh at her words. She had no idea. Instead, I dropped my head and nodded.

"I hope you have a better day," she said quietly.

I startled at the feel of her fingers on the back of my neck. I loved how they felt playing with my hair.

"Get some rest and drink lots of water."

Then she was gone. I listened to the pad of her footsteps walking through the apartment, not stopping anywhere, not investigating. She had to be the most un-curious woman I had ever met. I heard the sound of the door opening and shutting and the muted click of the automatic lock. I flopped back on the pillow, rolling and grabbing the one she had lain on, inhaling her sweet scent.

She had looked after me, was concerned. Her closeness had banished the dark and given me rest. Her touch eased the turmoil and brought me peace. I wanted her back there, in my bed, wrapped close to me. I wanted to feel her gentle touch again, soothing me.

I barked out a humorless laugh.

So much for not getting involved.

It was a long day of meetings and going through the raid the night before. As usual, I dressed in my suit, carried my gun and a secreted blade as I did when I had anything to do with Hidden Justice. It was an image the men relied on. When I was finally free, it was late evening, and I was restless. I drove my car around aimlessly, trying to clear my head.

Trying to stop myself from complicating matters any more than I already had.

I failed.

I lasted until ten o'clock, then I headed to the bar again, parking my car down the block. The seat I had sat in last night was empty, the bar busier this evening. A small group of bikers was in the corner holding court, loud, obnoxious, and insistent. I had noticed their bikes parked in front of the bar, some illegally on the sidewalk.

Tally was busy pouring pitchers of beer, filling orders, the other bartender busy as well. Tally's hair was in a long braid hanging over her shoulder, and I noticed she had on tights under her shorts. Her legs still looked spectacular. So did her ass. I slipped into the seat, waiting patiently until she found my gaze. Her eyes widened, and I shook my head, offering a silent promise not to repeat last night's behavior.

But I'd had to see her. I had struggled all day not to call her. Not to beg her to come see me. She had looked exhausted this morning, and I knew my behavior had caused a lack of sleep for her so I didn't want to disturb her. I was going to wait until Monday, but I didn't want this discussion to happen in the office, and I had finally admitted I couldn't even wait until Sunday.

She approached me, one eyebrow raised in question.

"Just a soda. And a cheeseburger when you have a moment."

"What are you doing here?"

"I was hungry."

She waited.

"I wanted to see you," I said simply. "To apologize."

"It's fine, Julian. I don't have time tonight. We're a waitress down, a busboy short, no proper security on the door, and we're all trying to cover. I have tables to serve. I'll put in your order."

I held up my hands. "No problem. I don't want to make your life more difficult."

"Hey, sweet cheeks! We're waiting over here!" a voice yelled out.

I turned and met the eyes of one of the bikers. He returned my glare with a curl of his lips, saying something to his crew, making them laugh.

"I hate bikers," Tally muttered, filling a tray with more pitchers of beer. "Especially this bunch. Every time they come in, they're a pain in my ass."

"You've dealt with them before?"

"We rarely get any of them in here, but sadly, yes. Brian usually watches them carefully, but I think Tom is more afraid of them. He lets them get away with too much. They're repugnant."

Anger began beating under my skin. "And they're bothering you?"

"Since the moment they came in." She tossed her braid over her shoulder. "Bikers," she said again, distaste in her voice. "The one who just yelled yanked on my braid so hard, it gave me a headache."

I grabbed the tray as she began to slide it away. "Let me."

"What?"

"Order my burger. I'll take this over."

"You can't."

"Oh, Ms. Wells." I smirked and winked at her. "You'll find I like nothing more than a challenge."

I stood, taking the tray with me. I approached the

group. They were a small bunch—brawny, tatted-up tough guys who liked to frighten women by acting like they were important. Command attention with their loud voices and overinflated egos.

I counted in my head. Six-to-one. I liked those odds. Especially given a couple of them had potbellies and looked older. I could take them easily. The "leader" of the group was about my age, mouthy and full of himself, and he was the one who had yanked on Tally's braid.

Unacceptable.

I slid the tray on the table as they all gawked at me.

"Where's the girl?"

"I'm helping. She's a little behind."

"I'd like her behind me," one of them muttered. "Or under me. I like the red ones. They fight."

"That won't be happening," I growled and leaned close. "In fact, you fine gentleman are going to finish your beers, tip the ladies well, and leave."

"Says who?" the one I had narrowed in on as being the leader snarled. "Who the fuck do you think you are?"

I lied. Convincingly. I tugged aside my jacket so they saw my holster, letting the fabric drop back into place casually.

"Well, aside from the fact that the redhead is under my personal protection, I'm the narc officer who can have a full team here in ten minutes, but before they arrive, take at least four of you out. I have a few other men in the bar who'll finish off the job, so I suggest you listen to what I say." I leaned on the table, my voice deadly cold. "If you don't want to risk it and spend the night in jail, wondering why your dicks are getting personal with the contents of your stomach, I suggest you do as I say. I already have your plates down, and I'm sure my other men will be happy to spend the night digging into your backgrounds. So, I suggest you shut up and leave." I stood straighter. "Enjoy the beer."

I sauntered back to the bar, typing in a message to Damien. His reply was swift.

Got it.

I picked up the ginger ale Tally had left for me, drinking the cold liquid. A moment later, Damien had what I needed. He'd tapped into the camera outside the bar, and now, I did indeed have their plates. I chuckled as he informed me two had outstanding warrants and he'd called in a tip to the cops. One way or another, the bikers' night was about to end.

I wasn't surprised when they drank their beer and stood, grumbling loudly about the service and shit beer, throwing money on the table, and stomping out. The leader was the last one out the door, glaring my way and flipping his fingers between us as if we had unfinished business. I gave him the one-finger salute and picked up my burger.

"What did you say to them?" Tally asked.

I shrugged. "I speak biker."

Tally laughed. "Another one of your talents?"

I heard the relief in her laughter. Saw the way her shoulders relaxed. Recalled her words. There was history there. I wondered if I would ever know it.

"One of many you've yet to discover."

A real, wide, beautiful smile curled her lips. "I look forward to figuring them out."

I was pretty sure I was forgiven.

I ate my burger, enjoying it thoroughly. I had no recollection of tasting it last night. The manager, Tom, came over and spoke to me.

"You're the guy who ran off the bikers?"

I wiped my mouth, preparing for a huge discord with him—chasing off business, etc. I planned on telling him what I thought of his management style. Or lack thereof.

"Yes."

"Thanks. Your bill is on the house. That group causes a lot of trouble. Whatever you said, I'm grateful." He walked away before I could speak my mind. I had a feeling he knew he was in for a dressing down.

"Damn," I muttered, turning back on the barstool and looking at my half-eaten burger. "I should have gotten rings with the burger."

Tally laughed. "I can add them."

"And a Guinness." At her raised eyebrows, I chuckled. "I'll sip it. But a burger without a beer—a free one? Come on, woman."

She poured me one, the head foamy and perfect, the dark ale bitter and satisfying on my tongue. She stepped into the kitchen, returning a few moments later with sizzling onion rings, laughing as I squirted ketchup on the plate beside them. I chewed and sipped, watching her. She was extraordinarily pretty. Even wiping the counter, collecting dishes, and pouring drafts, she drew my stare.

Tally stopped and refilled my soda, sliding it in my direction. I chuckled at her mothering ways but took a sip. "If you dislike dealing with bikers, or even the general public, why bartending?" I asked, curious.

She shrugged. "Sometimes you take what you can get. I had experience already. I had to eat and pay rent. I keep to myself here, so it works. The bikers are just my own personal, ah, thing. Otherwise, it's an okay gig."

I nodded in understanding, picking up my burger.

She disappeared through the door again with a trayful of dishes. I finished my burger and rings and pushed away my plate. I waited for her to return, my eyes never straying far from the door. The other bartender, Lillian, took my plate.

"Anything else?" she asked in a slightly bored tone.

A strange feeling took hold. One of worry and panic. I had no idea where it came from, but it was strong.

"Where's Tally?" I asked Lillian.

"Oh, probably on dish duty. We're all sharing tonight." She walked away, backing into the swinging door with her ass. "Or taking out the trash." She made a face. "We're sharing that too."

Something in me froze. The panic grew, my breath caught in my throat, and I was off my stool in seconds. Without waiting for permission, I barged through the swinging door, startling the staff.

"Taliyah," I barked.

The kid trying to tackle the pile of dishes jerked his head. "Trash. Taking her time too."

I was out the door he indicated in two seconds, my heart plummeting to my feet at what I saw.

Tally, terrified and crying, pressed against a brick wall, the leader of the biker pack crowding her, his hand gripping her throat.

The world around me turned red.

CHAPTER FIVE

Tally

I couldn't believe Julian had shown up again. Or the way he'd handled the bikers that had been a problem since they'd walked in. That group always was. They were too loud, too coarse, and lousy tippers to boot. If one of the other managers were here, I wouldn't worry so much, but Tom was inexperienced and gave them far too much leeway. Add in the fact that the security guy was useless, and it wasn't a good night. They made me uncomfortable.

The obvious leader of the group was obnoxious, lurid, and far too handsy. We were swamped, short-staffed, and the bar was busy. He let his displeasure at being kept waiting known—loudly—and had been rude when I got to the table. I had begged Lillian to switch tables with me since I already had a dislike of bikers, but she refused.

"Your problem, not mine," she muttered.

I had plastered a fake smile on my face and walked

over to take their order. For a moment, I thought I was overreacting. The one guy asked for three pitchers of draft and a large order of the hot wings. I nodded and turned away when I felt a hand on my ass. "I'd like this on my lap too," he sneered. "Sweet cheeks."

I spun around. "Not on the menu, asshole. Keep your hands to yourself."

I hurried away, trying to ignore their raucous laughter. It had only gone downhill. Tom, the manager on duty, was even worse than usual, barely keeping his head above water tonight with all the trouble that was happening. I dodged hands, closed my ears to the constant innuendos, and hoped the night would be over soon. It took all I had not to turn around and slap the biker who yanked on my braid to get my attention as I walked past delivering drinks to another table. My eyes smarted with the force of the pull, but I slapped his hand and walked away, muttering under my breath. I was going to talk to my boss about this.

Julian was like a knight in shining armor when he appeared. Whatever he said to the bikers made them leave, and when they departed, the sound of their motorbikes fading away, everyone relaxed. I was grateful for him stepping in and secretly pleased he had sought me out again. I wondered if he felt the same pull to me as I did to him, if he had shown up because, after last night, he was ready to address the elephant in the room. There was no denying the attraction between us. It was like a life-form of its own.

I headed to the kitchen to see what I could do to

help. Lillian could handle the tables for a while, and Julian was busy eating. Kevin, the kid trying to keep up with the dishes, indicated the bags by the back door. "Trash," he mumbled.

"I could do some dishes?" I tried. I hated trash duty. The back alley was dim, the trash container smelled, and I knew there were rats outside. I heard them scurrying, and it made my skin crawl.

"No, I'll finish. Dump those two bags, and we're caught up. I've been out three times already."

I kept my sigh to myself. Even Lillian had dragged out a couple bags earlier, so I supposed it was my turn. I opened the back door, scanning the alleyway. It was deserted, and I was grateful to see that at least the trash container lid was open. I only had to toss the bags and head inside. I grabbed the awkward, heavy trash, hurrying over, grimacing when the kitchen door shut behind me and the alley became darker. It creeped me out, and my breathing kicked up.

I tossed the bags one at a time, grateful neither of them split open. But before I could turn around, someone was behind me. I gasped in fright as I was pushed against the hard, cold brick wall and an angry voice spoke in my ear.

"Not so tough without your bodyguard, are you, sweet cheeks?"

I recognized his voice. It was the leader of the bikers. And he was furious.

I struggled against his hold, panicked. His hands tightened, the pain of his fingers digging into my arms burning. He spun me around, one hand going to my throat and squeezing as he slammed me to the wall with his other arm. My head hit the hard surface, the pain blooming in my skull, making me dizzy. His fetid breath washed over me, the scent of unwashed skin and old leather making me gag. "You think you're too good for the likes of me? Always ignoring me, pretending I don't exist?"

He pushed closer, cutting off my oxygen. "I'm gonna teach you a lesson you won't forget."

The world tilted in front of me, and I struggled to stay conscious. I knew if I passed out, I would end up somewhere else and at this man's mercy. One word echoed in my head, one plea that repeated itself.

Julian. Help.

It was like a mantra I couldn't stop. My fear morphed as the biker's fingers tightened and black spots appeared in front of my eyes.

Please, Julian.

Without warning, it happened. One moment, I was pressed into the brick, my shoulders screaming from the pain of the jagged cement digging into my skin and my lungs desperate for oxygen, and the next, a roar filled the alley and my assaulter was gone.

Julian stood over him, breathing fast, his face twisted into a menacing snarl. He held a knife in his hand, and the expression on his face was frightening.

He looked at me. "Go inside, Tally."

I couldn't get my legs to work. I was shaking so badly, I couldn't speak, move, or think. My head was muddled and confused. He seemed to understand that.

"Shut your eyes, then, baby. You don't need to see this."

My legs gave out, and I slid down the wall, pulling my knees to my chest and lowering my head.

I shut my eyes and tried to block out the sounds, failing completely. Groans and pain-filled gasps filled the air. The sounds of fists driving into flesh were repeated over and again. Julian's voice, cold, angry, and deadly calm, reached my ears.

"I told you. You didn't listen. She is under my protection, and now you've touched—*you've hurt*—what's mine. When you're pissing blood for the next week, remember this."

The biker groaned.

Julian cursed and muttered more threats. Angry words. I didn't dare lift my head.

I heard more muffled grunts, a low scream, and then silence.

Then Julian was in front of me. "Tally, it's me. You're safe now, okay?" He spoke soothingly, close to my ear. "I'm going to pick you up. Do you understand me?"

I nodded, still unable to speak. My fear was lodged in my throat as memories crowded into my head. Terror filled my chest, bringing panic and uncertainty with it. I gasped as he scooped me up, my body trembling and out of control.

"I have you, baby. It's okay. Everything is going to be okay."

There was a burst of activity and light as the door opened, and Kevin and Tom stepped into the alley.

"What the hell?" Kevin muttered.

Julian headed toward the door. "You're fucking lucky I came out. You should be sued for letting a defenseless woman step outside with no lights or protection," he snarled. "What kind of shithole place are you running here?" he raged.

"Is she-is she okay?"

"Does she fucking look okay? I'm taking her to the hospital."

"What about him?" Tom asked.

I dared to look. The biker was lying on the ground. There was blood on his face, and his arm was at a funny angle.

"Let the rats have him. The cops will pick up what's left of him," Julian ordered. "I'll handle it."

Julian opened a car door, sliding me in.

I grabbed at his hand. "No hospital."

"You need to be looked at."

"No hospital," I repeated. "I'm-I'm okay," I lied.

He cursed and shut the door, pulling out his cell. He stared at me as he spoke, then hung up, making another call. This time, he turned his back as he talked to whoever it was. I shut my eyes, remembering the look on his face in the alley. How dark and malevolent his expression had been. His eyes, cold and foreboding, his mouth twisted into a cruel smile. It was so at odds with the Julian I had come to know the past few weeks.

I knew I should be frightened by that side of him, yet I only found comfort in the fact that he had appeared. Grateful he had pulled the biker off me. Spared me from whatever awful plans he'd had in mind for me.

Julian slid into the car, starting the engine. He reached for my hand, and I flinched. He grimaced. "Don't be afraid of me, Tally. I won't hurt you."

"I know… I'm just…" I trailed off, unsure what to say.

"I know," he assured me. "But you're safe now, and no one is going to hurt you."

"Can you drive me home?" I whispered.

"I'm taking you to my place. A friend is meeting us there. She's a doctor and will examine you." His tone brooked no argument.

I was too tired to offer any.

The woman who examined me was kind and gentle. She introduced herself as Sofia. I winced when she probed my head, and I heard Julian cursing as she checked out my arms, back, and rib cage. I knew without looking that I was badly bruised. I could feel the blood pooling under my skin, the ache deep.

"Definite concussion. Contusions and bruising," she said with a frown. "I'd like a head CT." She patted my shoulder kindly. "You're going to be sore for a few days."

"Can you arrange the CT?" Julian asked. "Privately?"

"I can. Probably in a couple of hours."

"I'll get her there."

"What about…?" She trailed off.

"I'll take care of him as well."

It felt as if they were talking in code. I tried to follow the conversation, but my head felt heavy and I was so tired. My body ached.

A touch on my face made me startle, and my eyes flew open. I met Julian's concerned gaze, all the anger I had seen earlier gone. His amazing irises were muted and gentle.

"Tally, I have to take you for a test, okay? Sofia just wants to make sure you're okay."

"Is it far?" I asked. "I'm a little dizzy."

"I'll carry you."

"I want a shower." I grimaced. "I smell like the alley —like him."

"As soon as you've had your test and we get some pain pills in you."

"No hospitals," I mumbled, closing my eyes again.

"I promise."

I gave up and floated away.

JULIAN

Tally was in and out for the next while. Luckily, she stayed awake long enough for the CT Sofia had arranged in the old warehouse Marcus used to own. We used it as a second base now. Lots of my agents lived there and we kept the clinic stocked, and Sofia still worked on the men if needed.

Sofia was satisfied Tally wasn't in danger but wanted me to wake her every couple of hours to be sure. She got some pain meds into her, and Tally dozed all the way back to my place, her hand on mine as if making sure I was there. She didn't have to worry—I wasn't leaving her.

At my apartment, Tally leaned on me heavily, refusing to let me carry her. I took her to the shower, not caring as I got wet, helping get her inside and seated on the cedar bench in the stone-enclosed area. I stepped out and hurried to the closet, grabbing her a shirt and a pair of my boxers to change into. She was trying to wash her hair as I stepped back in, taking over. I tried to be as gentle as I could, but every whimper and flinch caused my anger to burn brighter again. That asshole was going to pay dearly for this.

I helped her clean her arms and legs, peeling off her shorts and tights, leaving her in her underwear. Once she was done, I washed my hair fast, clean enough from the water and soap I used on her. She stood, and I held the towel, averting my eyes as she removed the rest of her clothes and wrapped the towel around her body. She didn't object as I helped her from the shower to stand in front of the vanity.

"Stay," I ordered.

In my closet, I stripped and threw on a pair of sweats and a shirt, heading back to her. She was gripping the edge of the vanity, staring at her reflection in the mirror. I met her eyes in the mirror, the dazed and pained look in them tugging on my chest.

"I need to see your back," I said gently.

"My back?" she repeated.

"I need to see how bad the bruising is."

She frowned, and I covered her hand holding the towel to her chest. "Just loosen your grip. I won't hurt you."

"I know that."

She sighed and let the towel drop in the back. I wanted to slam my hand into the mirror at the mass of bruises and scrapes I could see on her pale skin. Her shoulders had taken the brunt of his aggression, and I knew she had to be sore—especially the right one, which seemed to have suffered the most. I lifted the cream Sofia gave me, showing it to Tally.

"This will help with the pain, but I have to touch you." I was certain she didn't want anyone, especially not a man, touching her right now, but her reply surprised me.

"I like your touch," she whispered, not meeting my eyes. "It's okay, Julian."

Unable to resist, I dropped a kiss to her shoulder. "You can call me Jujube if you want. Just for tonight."

My silly words made her smile for a second, then a sob escaped her mouth, and she lifted her hand to cover it.

"No, Tally," I hushed her. "Don't cover up your pain. It's okay."

I made fast work of the ointment, soothing it into the blemished skin then running my hands up and down her arms to cover those bruises as well. Sofia assured me there was not only pain relief in the cream, but it would help speed up the bruise healing as well.

Then I tugged up the towel and dropped my shirt over her head. She slipped her arms into the holes and allowed the towel to drop. Knowing she was too dizzy to do it herself, I slid my boxers over her feet, one at a time, and pulled them up her legs, trying not to react to the softness of her skin under my touch. How it felt gliding them over her full ass and slipping my fingers under the waistband to make sure it was flat. She never moved, didn't make a sound, and was surprisingly relaxed as I finished the job.

I was anything but.

I led her to my bed, letting her settle herself. She winced as she lay on her back, and I knew she was going to have trouble finding a comfortable spot for long.

"Your left shoulder isn't as bad," I suggested, watching as she eased to her side, then with a sigh, settled into the pillow, letting her eyes drift shut.

"I'll wake you in two hours," I murmured and began to leave, but her eyes shot open and she spoke, panicked and upset.

"Where-where are you going? Are you leaving?"

I sat on the mattress. "No, Tally, I'm right here. But I want you to rest. I'll only be in the next room."

She found my hand, her fingers gripping me tightly. "You won't leave?"

I didn't want to lie to her. "You will not be alone," I promised.

She accepted that easily enough, her eyes shutting once again.

For a moment, I was still. Then without thought, I lifted my hand, running it over her head. She made a sound low in her throat, but it was one of relief, not worry. I stroked her damp curls, whispering the odd reassurance as I watched her succumb to the medication and the exhaustion her body was feeling. Her grip never loosened on my hand, though, and I made no move to leave until I heard my apartment door open and I knew Damien had arrived.

I slowly extracted my hand and stood. Tally frowned but stayed asleep, and I left the room, leaving a light on and pulling the door shut.

In the living room, I found Damien and Sofia.

"How is she?"

"Asleep."

"How long?"

"Fifteen minutes."

She nodded. I glanced at Damien. "You have him?"

"He's at the warehouse."

"Awake?"

"At times. He keeps whining about his nuts."

I lifted one shoulder, recalling the swift, hard kick I'd planted in his crotch. It was probably going to ache like a bugger for days.

"What are you going to do with him?"

"Put the fear of God into him."

"Pretty sure it's already there."

"Just going to drive home the message."

Sofia shook her head. "I'm not covering up murder, Julian."

"Wouldn't ask you to. He's going to live. But he isn't going to bother Tally or any other woman again. Once I'm done with him, the cops can have him."

"You promise?"

"Yes. I'll be back before she wakes up and knows I was gone."

"I'll watch her."

"Okay. Let's go."

CHAPTER SIX

Tally

I woke up disoriented, aching, and exhausted.

Why was I so tired?

I tried to lift my head, but a gentle hand on my shoulder stopped me.

"What is it, baby? What do you need?"

I knew that voice.

I frowned in the dim light.

Why was Julian in my room?

There was a low chuckle. "I'm not in your room, Tally. You're in mine."

I tried to focus on the walls. I recognized the pictures from the other morning when I sat up all night making sure Julian was okay. Now, I was the one lying in his bed, my head on his lap. I felt his light touch running through my hair, gentle and even. I cleared my throat.

"I'm thirsty," I rasped out.

"Okay." He slid his hand under me, helping me to sit up. For a moment, the room spun, then it righted itself and Julian came into view. His beard was thicker, and he was bare-chested. His eyes were dark with worry, his brow furrowed as he studied me. He held a glass to my lips, and I sipped at the cold water gratefully.

"I need, ah, I need…" I trailed off and indicated the door to the washroom. Julian stood, holding out his hands, and he helped me from the bed. I swayed a little, then everything fell into place, and I shuffled to the washroom, Julian close behind me.

At the door, I paused, still confused and not sure what had happened.

"I've got it from here," I rasped.

He lifted his eyebrows. "I'll wait right here, then."

"I need some privacy."

"When you can walk on your own, know where you are, and can recite the alphabet backward, you get your privacy. Until then, I'm standing right here."

I blinked, unsure how to respond. He indicated the door. "I'll close it, but I'm not leaving. You are too unsteady."

He was right, so I gave in and went inside. As I passed the vanity, I looked at my reflection, stopping in horror. There were bruises on my neck—distinct fingerprints. When I pulled up the sleeves of the T-shirt I was wearing, seeing more bruises, a sob burst from my throat, and in an instant, the door flung open and Julian strode in. He saw me, his expression immediately softening. He stood behind me, wrapping his hands around my waist and pulling me close to his chest, his warmth and nearness welcome.

"They'll fade, Tally," he assured me, not offering

mindless platitudes or telling me it was okay. "And he won't get near you again. No one will hurt you again."

"My head hurts," I whispered.

"I'm not surprised. You hit that brick wall really hard. But it will ease as well. Tomorrow will be better."

I hung my head, unsure how to respond.

"I'll be outside. Call me when you're finished."

I nodded.

When he left, I looked up again, noting my bloodshot eyes and the scratches on my hands. I used the toilet, washed my face and hands, and brushed my teeth with a fresh toothbrush I assumed Julian had left for me. I ran my fingers through my hair, the jumbled mass of curls too much to try to fix, and I headed for the door. Julian was there, and I walked past him, then stopped, unsure where to go.

He strode to the bed and lifted the light blanket. "Back to sleep."

"I should go home and rest and stop taking up your time."

He lifted one eyebrow, waiting.

"I can't stay here."

He tugged on my hand, his touch gentle. "You can and you are."

I sat on the edge of the bed, and he sighed. Then he sat on the chair next to it and handed me some pills and more water.

"I'll rub more cream into your bruises, and you can go back to sleep."

"You kept waking me all night."

"Yes. Sofia wanted to make sure there were no

hidden problems with your concussion. You can sleep now, and I won't bother you."

"What about you? You must be tired."

He smiled, running a finger over my cheek, tucking a curl behind my ear. "I'll nap on the sofa."

"No. You take the bed, and I'll go to the sofa."

He scrubbed his face. "Are you always this stubborn?"

"Yes."

"I'm not leaving you alone. You rest better when I'm close."

"Then stay here with me."

He didn't say anything. Not while he rubbed cream into my skin, his touch gentle. Not while he watched me take the pills, his gaze intense. Not a word passed his lips as he lifted the covers and let me slide in, then lay beside me once he made sure I was comfortable.

When I shifted, he lifted his arm, letting me rest my head on his chest, his heartbeat a soothing rhythm under my ear. He wrapped his other arm around me, a low sigh leaving his mouth.

"Sleep, Tally. I'm right here. I've got you."

And I did what he asked.

Julian was gone when I woke up. I could tell he hadn't been awake long since the space beside me still held his heat. I slowly sat up, testing my body. I hurt, but it wasn't as bad as it had been. My head was clearer, although the pain in the back was still there. I used the washroom, ignoring my reflection as I brushed my teeth, then headed toward the living room. Julian was on the sofa, a cup of coffee in hand, staring out the window. He was still bare-chested, his sweats riding low on his hips as he stood.

"Hey," he greeted me. "How are you feeling?"

I cleared my throat. "Ah, yeah, a little better, I think." I ran a hand over my messy head, grimacing when my fingers touched the back. "What time is it?"

"Around three."

"Wow." I looked around. "Can you tell me where my clothes are?"

"In the laundry. You can have another shower if you want. I'll give you a fresh shirt to wear."

"I don't think I can walk home in just a shirt."

He frowned. "Who said you were going home?"

I swallowed. "Obviously, I have to go home, Julian. I haven't done any errands or shopping. I need to get ready for work tomorrow…" At the incredulous look on his face, I stopped talking.

"What?"

He set down his coffee and walked over to me. He stood close. Closer than he'd ever been. He lifted his hand, running his fingers through my curls. "The only place you're going, Tally, is back to my bed. You can shower, have something to eat, and get more rest. You need it to heal."

"I'll do that once I'm home."

"You aren't leaving."

"I can't go to work in your shirt either, Julian."

"Well, I would be fine with it, but I can understand your reticence," he teased.

I frowned. "I'm serious."

"So am I. You're staying here. You're not going to work tomorrow—in fact, I've closed the office for the day."

"But—"

He cut me off. "Do you really think after what you went through last night I'm going to let you out of my sight? Jesus, Tally, the sight of you...of that asshole hurting you?" He ran a hand through his hair. "It fucking killed me that he touched you. That he hurt you."

"You stopped him," I whispered.

"I got the most horrible feeling in my chest while I was sitting at the bar. Like you needed me and I had to find you," he confessed.

"I kept thinking about you. Begging you in my mind to come find me," I told him.

With a groan, he pressed his forehead to mine. "I felt your panic. I wish I'd come sooner."

"You saved me."

He pulled back, cupping my face. His eyes were a maelstrom of emotion. "I can't stand to see you in pain, baby. It rips my guts out knowing if I had been five minutes later—"

It was my turn to cut him off. "But you weren't. You got there."

He groaned low in his throat, resting his forehead to mine once again. "I want to be the one who is always there, Tally."

His words were spoken in a low, rough voice, as if they hurt him to admit. As if they had been torn from somewhere deep inside and he had no idea how to cope with them being spoken.

"Julian," I whispered. "What are you saying?"

"I feel something for you," he admitted. "I have from the moment you stepped into my office. I keep fighting it."

"Because I work for you?"

"That, plus, I'm older. And other things."

"So, we don't have a chance?"

He straightened, his eyes meeting mine. "You want a chance? Is that what you're telling me?"

"I feel something for you too."

Our eyes locked, the strong draw I had to him pulling at me. His hands were still on my face, his fingers moving restlessly on my skin.

"There are a lot of reasons I should walk away," he muttered.

"Are there any not to?"

His mouth covered mine.

"Yes."

JULIAN

Her mouth. Her sweet, I-want-to-see-her-smile mouth was perfect underneath mine. Soft, responsive, giving. I wrapped her close in my arms, careful not to press on her bruises. She melded to me, her pliant body fitting against me as if made to go there. I stroked along her tongue, the taste of mint and the sweetness that was Tally igniting all my senses. She whimpered and shivered, both in pleasure, sliding her arms around my waist and holding me tight.

I couldn't resist her any longer. The idea of her leaving today was unacceptable. The thought that I might have lost her before she even knew how I was feeling made me desperate. I couldn't risk her going. I needed her here where I could watch over her. No one could protect her the way I could, and right now, she was too vulnerable on her own.

I pulled back, dropping kisses to her cheeks, nose, and forehead, then taking her mouth again. I only meant to keep the kiss brief, but as soon as our lips touched, all bets were off. I slanted my mouth over hers, pulling her higher up my chest, deepening the kiss. She stroked the skin on my back in gentle passes. I grunted in approval, slipping my hand into her hair, feeling the tangle of curls, silky and rich, as I wrapped my hand around them. Time lost meaning as we drowned in the sensations and taste of each other.

One moment, we were standing. The next, I had her sitting on the counter, me between her splayed legs, as I tongue-fucked her mouth. The warmth of her center surrounded my cock, even with the layers of material separating us. She was a temptation I could no longer resist. There was no other word for her. Hotter, wetter, deeper—our kisses continued. Her injuries faded away, my worries evaporated, and nothing else mattered but this intense connection.

Until I tugged on her hair, and she stiffened. Realizing what I had done, I broke away, my breathing fast.

"Tally," I whispered. "Baby, I'm sorry. I got carried away. I forgot about your head."

She met my gaze, her blue eyes wide. The dull sheen of pain was gone, replaced by the brightness of passion. Her lips were swollen from mine, her cheeks flushed. Her harsh breathing matched mine.

I touched her cheek. "Are you all right?"

She smiled. Real. Wide. Lovely.

"Other than the fact that you stopped, yes."

"I hurt you."

"It's fine now." She leaned closer, pressing her hands into my back, inviting me to meet her halfway. "Where were we?"

It wasn't an invitation I wanted to resist.

So, I didn't.

Later, we were on the sofa, cups of coffee in our hands. She sat with her back against the armrest, her legs draped over my lap. I studied her, noting her occasional grimace, but other than that, she seemed all right.

"Stop looking at me as if I'm an experiment."

I chuckled. "Hardly that. I was a little, ah, handsy. I'm just making sure you're okay."

"I like your sort of handsy. It was last night's kind I object to."

There was something in her voice, a trace of bitterness that caught my ears.

"You've been subjected to that before?" I asked, keeping my voice steady.

She didn't say anything for a moment, then nodded.

"Can you tell me?"

"Not now."

She'd been through a lot, so I tamped down my curiosity.

"All right."

"It's pretty personal."

"So was my tongue down your throat, but we managed that well."

A smile tugged on her lips, and she huffed a laugh.

"I suppose we did." She took a sip of coffee before asking the question that had hung in the air since I'd pulled away from her.

"What's happening here, Julian?"

I paused before I answered. She had every right to ask that question. I only wished I knew the answer.

"I don't know."

"Bullshit."

I blinked at her vehemence.

"I'm sorry?"

"I hate being lied to. More than anything. Don't tell me you don't know what's going on here. You kissed me. You must have some vague notion of an idea in that sexy head of yours."

"Vague, yes," I agreed.

"Then say it."

I slapped my hands on my knees. She wanted honesty? She was going to get it.

"I'm your boss, older than you, not looking for a relationship, yet I can't stop thinking about you. Wanting you. And after last night, needing to protect you. I shouldn't have hired you because I was attracted to you the second you burst in the door, all flushed and pretty. I went against my own instincts and did it anyway. I was basically fucked then and even more so now because I can't seem to stay away from you. All I think about is having you. When you're close, I feel this odd sense of...peace. You calm me, and I'm selfish enough to want more of it. More of you." I drew in some much-needed oxygen. "I don't understand it, but that's it in a nutshell."

She blinked. Looked away, then back at me. "You think I'm pretty?"

It was my turn to blink. "That's all you got out of that?"

"No. I got it all, just clarifying."

"Yes, I think you're beautiful. Sexy. Adorable when you're rearranging your desk or taping my Post-it notes into place. All of it."

"Hmm. Was that so hard to admit?"

I started to laugh. This woman was crazy. Yet, as with everything else about her, I liked it. I leaned forward and kissed her nose. "Surprisingly, no."

"So, you think this is a relationship?"

I rubbed a hand through my hair. "I don't generally go around kissing women who work for me, so yes, I believe it's something."

"What about women you rescue?" she asked quietly.

I thought about the countless women Hidden Justice had helped. Would continue to help long after I was gone. Tally didn't know about them, though. She couldn't. It was too dangerous. She was just teasing me. I knew she was talking about herself.

"You are the single check mark in both those categories," I said.

"Ah," was all she replied.

"I work a lot. I get called to events, meetings, even out of town. I'm used to living alone, only thinking about myself—not answering to anyone. I'm not sure what sort of partner I would be. Relationships and I aren't exactly friends."

"Wow, you make it sound so fun. Irresistible, even."

I chuckled. "Just laying it on the line." I shifted closer. "But I'd like to try with you, Tally. I'm breaking every rule. Every single one of them, but I don't care. If you feel the same attraction I do, then tell me, and we'll figure it out."

"I don't kiss men who are my boss either. In fact, I can't recall the last time I kissed anyone."

"So, you're interested?"

She slid her hand into mine. "Yes, I am. I think you're incredible. Smart, caring, sexy. And how you looked after me last night?" She smiled again. "I can't thank you enough for saving me. Taking care of me. You made me feel as if I mattered."

"You do matter. You matter to me." I paused. "And you have to stay here—at least for a while. I need to look after you."

"Does that include kisses?"

I touched her cheek. "Yes."

"You sleeping with me, holding me?"

I shifted closer. "Yes."

"Ordering pizza from that guy? The good stuff?"

I laughed. I would order anything if she kept smiling and would eat. "Yes."

"Well then, you get your wish."

I kissed her, just because I could, then stood. "Pizza coming up."

After she nibbled on some pizza, she looked tired, and I insisted she lie down. She fell asleep quickly, and I did a little work, concentrating on some budget stuff I had been ignoring. I hated that part of the job, but it had to be done. An odd sound met my ears, and I swung myself in the direction of the noise. I hurried to the bedroom, not surprised to find Tally in the throes of a nightmare. I climbed in beside her, gently pulling her back to me and hushing her.

"Shh, baby, it's okay. I'm right here. You're safe. So safe with me."

She relaxed and seemed to drift back into sleep. I knew I should get up. Go work. Leave her alone. But I liked how she felt in my arms. The way she relaxed and curled her figure to align with mine. I stayed where I was, offering the warmth and protection of my body, not really wanting to move away, even though I knew I should. I relaxed, the sound of her breathing soothing. I hadn't slept much either last night, and I was tired.

I would just rest for a few moments.

I woke to the shadows of the evening. Tally's back was pressed against my chest, my arms around her. One of my hands was holding her breast, the nipple a taut peak in my palm. My face was buried in her neck, the skin soft under my mouth. My other hand was splayed on her stomach, two fingers pushed under her waistband. My cock was hard. Aching. Pressed against her. She had one leg bent, accommodating me. She whimpered, lifting her hand and grabbing the back of my neck. How we ended up tangled this way, I had no idea. I groaned at the feel of her, even though I knew I had to stop—no matter how good it felt.

"Tally, baby…"

She moaned low in her throat as my fingers flexed, teasing her nipple.

"Julian," she whispered.

"We have to stop. I can't. You're hurt. We can't—" The rest of my words were cut off with another groan as she undulated against me.

"Please," she whispered. "Make it go away. Make me feel good, Julian."

Of its own accord, my hand slid into the boxers she was wearing, finding her heat, the slickness warm and welcoming on my fingers. Imagining how it would feel on my cock made me curse. She lifted her leg higher, opening herself wider for my hand. I stroked and teased, touching and learning. I licked and kissed at her neck, tugged on her earlobe, my body a tight coil of desire.

"Please," she repeated. "Make me yours."

I gave in. The loose boxers slid off her in a second. I yanked down my sweats, barely breaking contact with her.

"Condom," I murmured.

"On birth control. Clean," she replied.

I slid my cock through her wetness. Groaned at the heat. Hitched her leg higher and notched myself at her entrance, ever aware of her injuries. Inch by glorious inch, I sank into her, slowly and carefully, until I was fully engulfed. Surrounded by her. She cried out as I slid my hand to her clit, stroking it lightly. I was desperate to move, frantic to thrust, to claim, but I knew I had to be gentle. I held her against me, rocking into her, pumping in and out in a slow, deep, steady rhythm, intent only on giving her pleasure. She whimpered and gasped my name. Clutched my hand that played with her breast. Pushed back against me. She turned her head, and we shared sloppy, uncontrolled kisses as I began to move and rock faster. She was tight and wet, her muscles clutching and pulsating. I touched her clit with more pressure. Buried my face in her neck as my orgasm began to build. Higher. Hotter. Faster. I wrapped my arm around her tighter, holding her close, and gave in to the sensation. Burning, twisting, rolling through my body like a wildfire out of control. She cried out, tightening around me, sending me into another spiral of ecstasy. We moved together until we were spent. Sated. Our bodies pressed together as if one, our breathing matching with long exhales. I kissed her neck.

"Okay, baby? Did I hurt you?"

"The opposite," she replied. "That was incredible."

"I didn't plan—"

She cut me off. "I know. Now stop ruining the moment and just hold me."

I nipped on her lobe playfully. "I'm still inside you."

"And what are you going to do about that?"

I laughed. "Another challenge, Ms. Wells?"

"You up to it?"

I nudged her. "What do you think?"

She wiggled her ass against me. "I guess we'll find out."

I pressed her flush to me. "Yes. Yes, you will."

CHAPTER SEVEN

Tally

I stepped from the shower, wrapping a towel around myself. At the vanity, I wiped off the condensation on the mirror, studying my reflection. The bruises were out, livid and dark on my neck and upper arms. My shoulders wore welts and more bruises, and they ached. Yet, despite my appearance, I felt relaxed and at ease.

Amazing, toe-curling orgasms did that for a girl.

As if he knew I was thinking of him, Julian appeared behind me. His gaze took in my injuries, and he dropped his head to my shoulder, kissing the marks. Then he met my gaze. "They'll fade."

"I know."

"I'll kiss them every day."

I lifted one eyebrow. "You think you'll have access every day, buddy?"

He leaned on the vanity, caging me between his arms. He pressed close, his breath ghosting over my skin as he kissed my neck, carefully sliding his hand into my hair to tilt my head for better access.

He skimmed his hands up my sides, his touch light, yet possessive. He skated his long fingers over the fold in the towel, tugging and loosening the cotton. He cupped my breasts, lifting and fondling the heavy mounds, then tweaked my nipples, the already hard buds becoming a focal point of pleasure as he caressed and played with them.

"If you weren't hurt, I'd fuck you right here," he breathed. "Prove *my access*."

"Your touch doesn't hurt," I moaned, ignoring the pull as I reached up my arms and gripped his neck. "You would never hurt me."

"Jesus," he muttered, meeting my eyes. "Don't tempt me, Tally."

I pressed back, feeling his erection.

"Please," I whispered. "You make it all go away."

He dropped his head back to my shoulder, sliding his hand back down my leg. He lifted it to the vanity and slid his fingers to my center. I let my head fall to his shoulder as he stroked me, pushing one finger inside. He groaned low in his throat.

"You're so wet. You want me."

"Yes."

"Right here?"

"Yes."

A moment later, he was inside me, his hand splayed across my hips as he drove into me. I had to rise up on my toes, whimpering in pleasure as he filled me.

"Watch yourself. Watch how you look when I'm inside you," he ordered. "How much you love my cock. How well you take it."

I stared at our reflection as he moved. One hand holding me close, the other plucking at my erect nipples, going from one to the other. The way his eyes watched us as I absorbed his thrusts, my body swaying in sync with his like a tree bending to the wrath of a windstorm. His eyes were glittering in the light, the gold vivid against the swirls of green and brown. They were focused on our image, turning him on even more. He gripped me a little tighter, picking up the pace, making me gasp as he hit a place inside me I never knew existed. He dropped his other hand back to my clit, circling it and ratcheting up the pleasure.

Everything faded away. Nothing hurt, nothing ached. There was only him. The feel of his touch, the sensation of his skin on mine. His hot breath on my neck, his muttered curses and dirty words. The way he was transfixed on our reflection. On watching me watch us. I turned my head, and he caught my mouth— demanding and hard, his tongue twisting with mine. He became faster, almost frantic, holding me hard against him.

"Watch me come inside you. Watch how beautiful you are when you orgasm," he demanded, turning my head. His eyes went dark, narrowed with pleasure as he groaned. Fire raced down my spine, exploding and carrying me away. I cried out his name, the sound echoing off the tiles. I clutched his neck, holding on to him, desperately needing him to ground me.

He rode me until he was done. Until I was sated, the last of my orgasm trembling tendrils that shook me. He wrapped his arms around me, kissing my damp skin. I met his eyes, the fire now a low, banked flame.

"We both need another shower," he murmured.

He pulled my leg off the vanity, rubbing at the skin. "Okay, baby?"

"Yes."

He kissed my shoulder. "I knew you were going to be trouble." Then he kissed it again. "The very best kind."

"What are you reading?" I asked.

Julian glanced up from his book. "Beating up Bikers for Dummies. It helped a lot."

I burst into unexpected laughter at his silliness. With a grin, he picked up his scotch, sipping it.

"Laughter and a smile. Epic day," he said. He held up his book. "A biography. Pretty dull, actually."

We were quiet for a moment.

"Why did you have a knife?" I asked. "I saw a gun too."

"I'm always armed when on the job."

I frowned. "There was nothing on the schedule last night."

"I was doing a private job."

"You do those a lot?"

"Yes."

"You beat him up badly."

"He deserved it," he said, his tone firm.

"Is he…dead?"

He gaped at me. "Why would you ask me a thing like that?"

"Your face in the back alley. You were so—" I shook my head, unable to find the right words. "You looked lethal. Dangerous."

He frowned and stayed quiet, as if contemplating his words. Then he shook his head.

"No. He's in police custody."

My heartbeat picked up. "Will I-will I have to testify?"

"No. I took care of it. They're holding him on other charges. His little group of friends is effectively done. He won't be out for a while, and their clubhouse was raided. They're all up on charges, singing like birds to try to protect themselves and get a deal." He snorted. "Not an ounce of loyalty among them, but I suppose I shouldn't be surprised."

I had to agree. I gazed at him in wonder. He was always a step ahead on everything. Thought of everything, it seemed.

"Thank you," I breathed out, wanting him to know how grateful I was.

His next words shocked me, though.

"I'm hiring you full time."

"What?"

"I don't want you going back to that bar."

I shook my head. "Julian, you can barely keep me busy three days a week, never mind the fourth you already added."

He shrugged, pulling on my feet and placing them on his lap. "I'll find other duties for you. I hate budget stuff. You can handle that. Plus, you can help Leo. And you can use the time to work on school stuff."

"You can't pay me to take courses."

"Stop arguing with me. It's happening."

I crossed my arms. "Julian—"

He locked stares with me, neither of us willing to back down.

"You can't pay me for doing nothing. I'm not a charity case."

"I never said you were. Don't put words in my mouth." He scrubbed a hand through his hair. "Listen, I can't let you go back to the bar. I doubt any of them would come around there again, but I can't risk it. You're safe in my building. You can work, do your schoolwork—" he flung out his hand "—clean this place every week if it makes you feel better, but that is what has to happen."

"I'm not your responsibility."

In a second, he was beside me on the sofa, crowding me into the corner. "That's where you're wrong. You became my responsibility the second you walked into my office. You became my friend the moment you chose to care for me and sat up all night watching over me." His voice softened and became low and husky. "You became *mine* the instant my lips touched yours and you let me into your sweet body. So, you can't tell me not to worry or think that we can go back to the way things were before this weekend." He cupped my face and kissed me. Long, slow, and passionately. "Because that is not happening. I'm not fighting it anymore. You're mine, so get used to it."

He kissed me again and picked up his book but didn't move away. He kept his hold tight on my legs as if I would run away.

I could barely move in shock at his little speech. I should be jumping up and telling him off. Refusing him. Being involved with him was dangerous. I needed to tell him no.

Instead, I muttered, "Bossy much?" under my breath.

He squeezed my legs. "You love it."

"Shocked with all that oozy, subtle charm, you're still single." I sniffed. "Lucky me."

He chuckled. "Grumble all you want. It's still happening."

I shut up.

Because, really, I rather liked being his—at least so far.

Later that night, we lay in his big, comfortable bed, a lamp in the corner casting its dim glow across the room. It had started to rain earlier, the sound of the water hitting the glass a low noise in the background. We faced each other, his hand on my hip, his other arm tucked under his head, mimicking my position. Dinner had been another takeout, and when I questioned Julian about his fairly empty cupboards, he shrugged dismissively.

"My schedule is erratic. Plus, I don't cook well, so it's easier to do takeout."

"That's something I could do. I'm a decent cook. I could shop and make you meals. Easy stuff you can reheat. Plus, you should keep some things on hand. Soup, that sort of thing."

He had kissed my forehead, smiling. "Whatever you think."

I had to do something. I had been serious earlier when I told him I wasn't a charity case.

I shifted and he frowned. "Are you all right?"

"I'm fine. A little achy but fine."

He ran his fingers down my cheek. "You're strong. Brave." He smirked. "Sexy in my shirt. Even sexier out of my shirt."

"I have to go home tomorrow."

"I'll take you and get some of your things."

I frowned. "You can drive me home, but I'm staying there."

His lips tightened, but he didn't argue. I wasn't sure if I was disappointed or not. I had to admit, I liked it there—with him. The building you couldn't get into without a pass card for the elevator or walking past the concierge. The heavy doors and locks. Plus, him.

Julian.

He had made love to me again, this time face-to-face, our bodies moving together with an ease that shocked me. I had never enjoyed sex as much as with him. It was as if my body was attuned to his and we knew exactly how to bring the other pleasure. His touch was warm, his mouth addictive, and what he did when he moved inside me? Explosive. He took away the hurt, the pain, the constant worry. They evaporated, and the only thing left was him. Us. I had never experienced anything like it.

He studied me, then spoke, his question like a sudden explosion in the room.

"What are you hiding from, Tally?"

I felt the color drain from my face.

"What?"

"Something from your past has you scared. Tell me and let me help."

There was nowhere to run. To hide. He was too close, his arm draped over my hip holding me there. His eyes saw too much, and after the other night, I knew he deserved an answer.

"My dad died when I was a baby. My mom passed when I was older. I lived with my grandmother."

"In Quebec."

"Yes."

"My half brother lived there too."

"Half?"

"My mother had been married before she met my dad. I was ten years younger than Dean. He lived with his dad until he passed, then he went to my grandmother's. He was never very close with my mom. They argued a lot, from what I understood."

"Were you close to him?"

I smiled sadly. "He was a good brother. Or at least he was until he started hanging with a biker gang."

"Ah."

"They came around one night and pushed me around a little, scared me."

"Fuckers," he growled.

"He left their gang but took up with another one—

and they were worse. He got caught up in some bad stuff. It changed him. Even my gran noticed."

He nodded. "That explains your dislike of bikers."

My throat became thick, my vision clouding as tears built. "Dislike isn't a strong enough word. Hate is more like it."

"What happened, Tally?" he asked quietly.

"They killed him," I whispered.

JULIAN

I stared at her, aghast. I hadn't expected that answer. I wasn't sure what had made me ask her about her past at that exact moment. Except she was soft and warm, pliant and relaxed after our lovemaking, and I hoped she would open up to me. And when she mentioned she had to go home the next day, I saw the flicker of fear return to her eyes. Felt her body stiffen slightly at the thought. I wanted to know why.

"Baby…" I tightened my grip.

"I was seventeen when I went to live with my grandmother. Dean was twenty-seven. He lived over the garage at Gran's when I first got there. I had hoped to get to know him better, but he was pretty private. We got along well enough. He tried to help —he was always nice to me. He told me jokes and made me laugh. It was a hard adjustment for me, but I pushed through. I went to school, graduated, then took a couple years off to save money. My parents didn't have much, and all my gran had was her house and her little pension. We lived very frugally."

She shifted, wincing a little at her shoulder.

"I always knew I wanted to come here to study art. I worked and saved for the tuition. Dean became more and more distant. He moved out of Gran's, and we hardly ever saw him. He'd drop by on occasion at the bar I worked at, but he never came to the house. And he never stayed long. He'd give me money for Gran and check up on me."

"What did he do?"

"He was a mechanic."

She wiped under her eyes. "The last few times I saw him, he was different. Cold. He didn't look well. But he refused to tell me what was going on. Then my gran got sick, and she died—it happened really quickly. She left him the house in the will, but she told him she wanted me to have half if he decided to sell. And I could live there rent free until I went to school."

"I'm surprised she didn't spell it out in her will."

She shrugged. "She had made it years before I came to stay with her. Like I said, he and my mom never got on. He went to live with Gran when I was about three, so she was very close to him. I think that was her way of looking after him. She figured I had my parents, so she became his. She never changed the will, but she sat us down and told us what she wanted. Dean had no problem with it, so there was no need to change the wording, I suppose."

"So, what happened with the house?"

She looked lost in a memory for a moment, the sadness in her eyes getting deeper.

"I decided it was time to go to school, and Dean didn't want the house. It was a little out of town and run-down. He had an appraiser in who said the house needed to be torn down, and the land wasn't worth much where it was. 'Just a bit of scrub brush,' he called it. Dean got a second opinion, who basically said the same thing, although he was a little more polite. It wasn't a big plot, and all around, it wasn't developed. So, he didn't get much for it, but my share would let me go to school and not work, at least for a while."

"But?" I asked, sensing the crux of the story coming.

"Dean told me my gran had taken out a loan against the house. He took the proceeds from the sale after he repaid the loan and put it into the bank. But I found out that he, ah, he liked to gamble. And he decided he could make us more money. He gambled away his half—" she sighed, the sound despondent "—then he did the same with mine, certain his luck would change."

I cursed silently. The stupid bastard.

"When he lost it all, he borrowed from the bikers he hung with, certain he could win it back. He just needed a little more time."

This time, I couldn't stay quiet. "Jesus. What an idiot."

"I think he was set up. He told me he doubled it at one point…" She trailed off.

"And then lost it," I guessed.

"Yes. He had a little left, but not much."

"So, they came after him."

"They beat him up pretty bad. He looked terrible. They accused him of holding back. They'd heard rumors from his former gang that he had a sister, and they told him I could be used to pay the debt back."

I pulled her closer, horrified. "*Fuck*. Tell me it didn't happen, baby."

"Earlier that week at the bar, a bunch of bikers had come in. They kept staring at me, talking among themselves. One of them followed me to the storeroom and pinned me against the wall, and he told me they were watching. He told me to tell Dean, 'They liked what they saw.' The guy roughed me up a little. It scared me, and I told him what they said and showed him the bruises. He got really upset and said it was nothing compared to what they could do. What they would do once they found out everything about me. He gave me some money. Told me to disappear. Get out of the province. He suggested Alberta, saying I could get lost there. Not to contact him. To never come back to Quebec." She sighed. "He went by his father's last name, so they didn't know who I was yet, and he thought if I left and they couldn't find me, they would figure something else out. He'd kept our lives so separate. It was the first time I realized he was doing it to protect me and my gran. What he didn't think about was that it hurt us since we didn't understand. Sometimes, the truth is better."

I ignored the flash of guilt her words caused. The secret I was keeping from her was different.

"So, I left that night. I packed a bag and took the first bus I could get."

I pulled her a little closer. "Tally, you must have been so frightened."

"I was, but I met a girl my age on the bus. I liked her and we talked. I didn't tell her everything except I was alone and needed a place to stay. She said she was getting off in Toronto. She told me she knew of a room for rent. And her aunt ran an office cleaning service. For the next two years, I hid. I worked nights cleaning offices, slept in a little room in the basement of her aunt's during the day. I rarely went out." A shiver ran through her body. "June and her aunt Cathy were very kind, but everywhere I looked, I saw danger. Every stranger I met was a potential threat. June and Cathy knew I was in some sort of trouble, and Cathy paid me cash under the table and took the rent off it. I had no bank account—nothing. I paid cash for everything. Only used the internet in cafés." A sob escaped her throat. "I found out my brother had died in a newspaper article I saw not long after I got here."

I pressed a kiss to her head. "I'm sorry, Tally."

"Eventually, no one seemed to be looking for me. I was tired of it all. I finally decided I'd hidden long enough, so I enrolled in school. Found another little place to live closer to school. Worked tons of odd jobs to pay for everything. And stayed in the shadows. Always still afraid, but tired of not living."

"If they killed him, he was probably right. They didn't find out who or where you were, and he paid the ultimate price. But you're good to be cautious." I paused. "Do you remember the name of the group?"

"Belham Terrors." She shivered again. "I'll never

forget it. I only found out because I saw him in a jacket once that had the patch on it. Two dogs ripping each other's throats out. The men in the bar had worn the same jacket." She shut her eyes. "I never mentioned it to him. I never understood why he was part of them. He wasn't like that. He became a different person. He did drugs, he drank, he…he made terrible decisions…" She trailed off. "I lost him a long time ago, I suppose."

I didn't know what to say to her. Knowing how scared she must have been. How alone. Yet, still pushing forward, keeping her head down, and going on with life. She was incredibly brave and strong.

"Do you see your friend anymore?"

She didn't meet my eyes. "People drift, and sometimes it's for the best."

I hated knowing how alone she was.

"That's why you like the building," I said. "Why you wanted to work for me."

"Yes, I feel safe there."

"You are. You're safe there." I wrapped her in my embrace, holding her tight. "Here—with me. Nothing will happen to you when you're with me."

"I know," she whispered. "I always feel safe with you."

The words were out of my mouth before I could stop them. "Then stay."

She looked up. "What?"

"Stay here with me."

"What—live here?"

"Yes."

She looked confused. "In the guest room?"

I chuckled. "You really think I want you in the guest room? I want you here in my bed."

"I can't, Julian. It's too—"

"Fast? I know. Stupid? Undoubtedly. Rash and unlike me? Totally. But it also feels right. I miss you when you're not in the office. When you are, I find excuses to get close, and I hate it when you leave. Knowing what I know now, I can't let you go back to being on your own."

Worry made her frown. "Do you think I'm still in danger?"

"Since it's been so long, no. But you've been alone too long. I've been alone too long. I want you here, and why should we wait?"

"Because normal people would."

"So, we're not normal."

Still, she hesitated. "I need to think about it."

I loved and hated the fact that she said that. She was proud and independent, which I loved, but I hated that she might say no, when the thought of her on her own made me anxious.

"Not for too long."

I held her long after she fell asleep. I needed to get Damien on the search for that biker group. Make sure she was safe. Protect her at all costs. If they were okay with the idea of whoring out someone's sister, God only knew what else they were capable of doing. Hidden Justice could shut them down. Punish them.

I had never felt such a personal need for justice before now. But then again, I had never fallen—

I caught myself before I let my brain spew out the words.

I wasn't in love with Tally. It wasn't possible.

I looked down at her, asleep and safe in my arms.

Was it?

CHAPTER EIGHT

Julian

It was impossible not to notice how anxious Tally was the next day when I drove her to her apartment. Located downtown in a busy, crowded neighborhood, I had trouble finding a parking spot—one of the many difficulties of living in such a hectic area. Finally, after circling the block several times, I managed to find one, and I parked the car. Following her, I saw the tense set of her shoulders and the way her head moved back and forth as if searching for danger. I stepped to her side, drawing her close.

"No one will touch you."

I felt her shuddering breath and squeezed her waist. She looked better this morning, her coloring returning to normal, and more rested. The bruises showed up on her creamy skin, but her voice wasn't as raspy. She would heal—I would make sure of it.

I looked around her tiny place, trying not to show my distaste. One room with a bathroom in the corner, hidden by a door. A makeshift kitchen with a toaster oven and hot plate. Her bed pushed against the wall, piled with cushions to act as a sofa as well. A dresser beside it, chipped and worn. A tiny table with one chair tucked under it. The solitary chair spoke to me, its singleness a reminder of how alone in the world she was. A small rolling metal rack served as a closet.

I looked around and made a decision. She wasn't coming back here. Ever.

Tally looked at me. "What?"

I had spoken my thoughts out loud.

"Nothing." I knew she'd fight me on it, and I didn't want to fight with her today.

"I heard you." She slammed her hands on her hips, glaring at me. There was a spark in her eye and a defiant scowl on her face. Color saturated her cheeks, and she was determined. Furious at my unsolicited decision. She was extremely sexy when she was pissed at me. My cock thickened at her incensed beauty.

Maybe I did want to fight.

"Take what you need for now. I'll come get the rest later."

She stepped closer, the pissed-off kitten becoming a lioness.

She poked me in the chest. "I don't think so, asshole. You can't just walk in here, make a decision based on your snotty ideas, and expect me to fall in line with it." She poked me again. "You're not the boss of me."

I took her hand, lifting it to my mouth. I kissed the palm, then turned it over, kissing the knuckles.

"I think you're wrong there, Tally. I am your boss." I tugged her a little closer. "And you like it."

"You can't tell me what to do," she hissed, trying not to give in. But I saw the way her eyes darkened, and her voice wavered a little.

I kissed her wrist, letting my tongue graze over the tender skin. "You're coming home with me, and you're not coming back here."

"Maybe I don't want to stay with you." Her voice wobbled a little.

I dragged her to my chest, lowering my head and kissing the edge of her mouth, feeling the way her lips trembled. "I think you do."

Her fingers flexed on my shoulders.

"I think you want to come home with me. But first, I think you want me to toss you on that little bed over there and fuck you," I whispered in her ear, nipping at her lobe. "Give you one good memory of this place."

She whimpered, and I covered her mouth with mine, kissing her until she was shaking in my arms. I stumbled back, falling on the bed, taking her with me so she was on my lap. Her legs splayed wide, surrounding me, and I groaned at the heat of her. She wanted me as much as I wanted her.

But the sudden weight on the bed proved to be too much, and before I knew what was happening, the frame gave away and we were on the floor, jolted and stunned. She was over me, shock registering on her face as our eyes locked. Then she began to giggle. I started to laugh. She buried her head into my neck, her amusement getting louder. I held her tight, sharing it with her.

Finally, she lifted her head, and I cupped her cheeks. Her eyes were sparkling in humor, she was relaxed and at ease, and my breath caught in my throat at her beauty. I wanted to see her like this all the time.

"Come home with me, Tally. Stay. I don't want you here. I want you with me."

"Was that so hard to ask?"

I lifted one eyebrow, waiting until she nodded.

"Fine," she breathed out. "But I'm not giving up my lease. I just paid for this month."

That was fine. I would make sure by the end of the month, she had no desire to come back here. I already knew by the end of the month, I wouldn't let her go.

———

The next morning, secreted in my hidden office, I watched Tally. She wore one of her pretty dresses, her hair down today. An artful scarf was draped around her neck, covering the bruises. The sleeves of her outfit hid the ones on her arms. The only things still visible were her movements, which were a little slow, but most people wouldn't notice. A small grimace of pain would cross her face if she tried to lift her arms too high. It was already easier for her, but I still hated to see it.

Yesterday, after we'd picked ourselves up off the floor, I put the old frame back together while she gathered some clothing and personal items. On the way out the door, I swiped most of the clothing off the metal rack she used as a closet and put it in the trunk with the bag she had packed. I was amused when she carried out a pile of cushions.

"Your place is so sterile," she said by way of explanation. She added the blanket from her bed. "My gran made me that."

I didn't really care what she brought, as long as it meant she was there. Watching her arrange the cushions on my leather sofa had been amusing, though. In the end, she had put them in the guest room, deciding they didn't "go at all." I promised her we could pick other cushions together.

I flicked off the monitor and turned to the task at hand. Using an untraceable line, I had a face-to-face call with Matteo and Marcus. It was later in the day in the part of the world where they lived. We exchanged pleasantries, and I had to smile at the sound of children's voices in the background and Evie calling to them. Matteo grinned, not at all apologetic.

"Bedtime." He chuckled dryly. "Always a production. I never knew how imperative a glass of water could become. Any delay, actually."

Not wanting to take up much of their time, I asked some questions about biker gangs and their thoughts and any dealings they'd had with them. Matteo frowned, shaking his head.

"Most of them are lower-level crimes. Drugs seem to be their thing, not slavery or selling women and children, so they were never on our radar. The RCMP are usually on top of them. The worst ones are given priority. Why the sudden interest in a biker gang?"

I hesitated then told them. They exchanged a glance, then Marcus spoke.

"You have a personal interest in this woman?"

I scrubbed my hand over my face. "Yeah, I do."

"She is, ah, important?"

I hesitated. "Yeah, she fucking is." Then I couldn't shut up. "I hired her even though I knew I shouldn't. It was as if someone else had taken over my mind and body. I couldn't stop thinking about her. I felt like a fucking stalker. And it's only gotten worse."

I rubbed my eyes and told them what had occurred on the weekend. How she cared for me. The attack. My reaction. The intensity of what I felt for her. The gist of her story.

Marcus grinned. "Lightning again, Julian?"

I met their eyes, serious. "I would kill for her. Without thought."

Matteo's eyebrows shot up. "Then keep your head in the game, Julian. Find out what you can, but if they aren't a threat to her, leave it alone. Don't start a war you don't need to. Leave them to the RCMP and their fate. If they're a danger to her, then you know what to do, but do it properly."

"I can't stand the thought of any threat to her," I admitted. "Jesus, how did the two of you handle this shit? I feel as if I'm going to come out of my skin. I want to lock her up in a room and never let her out."

They both had the nerve to laugh. "Now you understand our reactions."

Matteo leaned closer to the camera. "Bring her here.

She would be completely safe. Evie and Missy would befriend her."

"And what the hell am I supposed to do without her?" I snapped without thinking.

Marcus shook his head. "It's simple, Julian. If you love her—and I think you do—you give up that life and make a new one with her. Here."

I stared at the screen in silence.

"We all find our reason," Matteo said. "We all reach that point where we want more than we can get from fighting a never-ending battle. We have to let others carry on while we choose a different path. If you aren't ready now, you will be soon. Think it over."

I nodded, still silent.

"Bring her here for a vacation. See how it feels. You would be welcome."

Damien entered the room and stopped to say hello to them as I sat, my mind racing. I ended the call, their words echoing in my head. I shook it to clear the thoughts and focused on Damien.

"What did you find?"

He shook his head. "They're a bunch of scum. Drug dealers, into loan-sharking, prostitution. The women all appear to be of age, though." He lifted a shoulder at my inquisitive stare. "I can't say if they're willing or not. The club keeps a pretty low profile. They've been raided, charged, let off, got a slap on the wrist, and done it all over a few times. Nothing seems to stick much." He rubbed his chin. "But there's something there. I can feel it. I need to dig more."

"Any information on Tally's brother, Dean?"

He tapped on his keyboard. "Well, since their online security was for shit, I was able to get right into their system. They keep lousy records, although I found a few things. There is a Dean Bedford. Long list of charges. He's the leader of the group. Usurped the old one."

Damien looked up. "Funny enough, the old leader has never been seen since Dean staged a coup."

"Has to be a different Dean. Her brother's dead."

Damien spun his laptop. "Is he?"

I stared at the picture on his screen. The picture of the biker wouldn't have caught my eye except for one thing. The wild copper hair. Even with it brushed back and wrapped in a bandanna, Dean's bright hair color was still visible. I narrowed my eyes, studying the picture. That was the only similarity. It had to be a coincidence. This man was rugged, with a heavy beard. Cold, dark eyes. Again, my gaze went to his hair. It set him apart from the other bikers.

Something was wrong. Something didn't add up in this story. It had felt odd when Tally told it to me, and now something was screaming at me.

"Find out everything you can on him. I don't want to chase shadows."

He nodded, his eyes focused on the screen. After a while, he looked up, his gaze serious. "He isn't a shadow, Julian. Tally's mother was married to a man named Trevor Bedford. Her father was Wells. I can't find an official death certificate for anyone by the name of Dean Bedford."

"Tally read of her brother's death in the paper."

"And we all know everything you read in the paper is

true," he said sarcastically. "Maybe he planted it, knowing she would see it."

He was right.

"This makes no sense."

He cracked his knuckles. "It will when I'm done."

I nodded, knowing he was right.

How was I going to tell Tally?

Three days later, it did. The entire sordid story made sense. Dean wasn't the nice guy caught up in the wrong crowd Tally thought him to be. Her trust and love had been misplaced.

Dean had a long string of crimes against him. Including swindling. The "bit of scrub brush" he'd told Tally it was had been worth a lot of money. Over a million bucks. Her grandmother had owned all the land around her house, not just the piece the house sat on. He'd obviously had people lie about the value. He'd made up the whole story about gambling it away. The gang coming after her. Protecting her. The greedy bastard had frightened her into running and living in fear for years. Mourning his death.

And he was very much alive.

And he ran a dirty, criminally active bike gang. Drugs and prostitution were rampant. Unsolved murders were attributed to them, including that of the ex-president of the club, but never proved. It had been a fairly low-level club until Dean took it over. Now the members were a law unto themselves. We studied the records, the revenue. All the top members were wealthy. Living high.

It took Damien and me an entire day to realize how often the top members of the club changed. And each time, Dean became richer when they disappeared.

Her half brother was a piece of work. And he needed to be stopped.

I sat with the evidence surrounding me. RCMP had done nothing. They were never able to make charges stick.

"Inside man," Damien mused.

"Feels like it."

"What do you want to do?"

I scrubbed my face. "I don't know."

"Do you think Tally is a target still?"

I tapped a picture of Dean. "He doesn't leave loose ends. I fear Tally is alive because he hasn't found her. He told her to go to Alberta. If he isn't looking here now, he will be soon. If he does…" I trailed off, unable to say the words.

"He could have killed her instead of making her scared enough to run."

"She's his sister. I think a few years ago, that counted for something. The man he's become, I'm not so sure."

"A great deal of missing women are linked to his club." Damien met my eyes. "I think he's starting to dip his toes into dangerous territory. Territory we can't ignore. I've been watching video surveillance around his clubhouse. There's an awful lot of activity for some bikers meeting for beers and to discuss their rides. The money they control is scary."

"Maybe it's time we step in. I need to ascertain if she's still in danger."

"Will you tell her?"

I barked a laugh. "That the man she thought of as her big brother lied, cheated, and stole from her? Allowed her to live in fear for the past few years without a second thought?" I shook my head. "If he'd handed her the fifty thousand he'd told her was her share of the house sale, she would have left. Never bothered him except a call or Christmas card. But the greedy, selfish bastard wanted it all, so he made everything up. I bet he even sent the bikers to rough her up and scare her—add credence to his story. The lowlife gave her a few grand and sent her off on her own, scared and thinking she was all alone. I want some answers from him, then I'll tell her."

"You'll have to tell her about Hidden Justice, then."

"I know. When I'm ready."

He stood. "Don't wait too long, Julian. Sometimes things happen and our decisions are taken away from us. Omission is another form of a lie. She's had enough of those."

I nodded. "I know."

"Give me some time to dig into everything. Then we can figure out our plan."

"I'll bring in the local team, and we'll join them."

"Not until I know everything. The setup, the escape routes, what I think we're dealing with."

He was right. We weren't going to rush into this. Tally was safe, and we needed to be sure of everything before we stepped in. "I'll call the team leader in

Montreal and fill him in. You can link up with their guy and get us everything we need. We'll get eyes on them."

He left, and I shook my head.

When I thought Tally would be trouble, this wasn't what I was thinking. I'd had no idea.

But I would make her safe, no matter what.

CHAPTER NINE

Julian

"Chop those onions." Tally pointed to the cutting board. "Finely."

"You always give me the worst jobs," I grumbled, picking up an onion to peel it.

"I took over handling the tenants and all the damn paperwork that entails at the office," she shot back. "That's the worst job there is."

I didn't hide my grin. It was. And she was already doing better than I ever could. Her meticulous, orderly mind-set was a benefit. It filled in her hours and took a lot off my plate. And the tenants loved her. Leo enjoyed working with her.

"I want the carrots sliced, not diced, when you're finished with those." Sarcasm dripped from her voice. "This week, preferably."

"Bossy much?"

"You boss me around all day," she sniffed. "It's my turn."

I leaned over and nipped her neck playfully. "You

love it when I boss you around." I indicated the pile of vegetables waiting for me. "There're a lot, so shut it."

"There're a few onions and carrots. Suck it up, buttercup."

I sighed heavily and purposely slowed down.

She waited only a few more moments before nudging me out of the way and doing the task herself. "Slowpoke," she muttered. "I'd like to eat tonight."

I stood behind her, linking my arms around her waist. She was faster—far more efficient than I was—with her knife skills. Luckily, not in the same way Marcus's wife, Missy, was. I'd have to duck a lot if Tally could toss a knife with the deadly accuracy Missy could.

"I like watching you in the kitchen," I murmured into her ear, ghosting my lips down her neck. "You're so sexy in an apron, making dinner."

She shivered, and I smiled against her skin. I loved these evenings with her. In the apartment, where we were simply Julian and Tally.

I adored having her here. I had never understood Matteo's or Marcus's need to spend so much time with the women they fell for. But that was before Tally. Even with her in the office during the day, I found myself longing for the hours spent away from business, just to be able to be with her. To listen to her talk, to hear her low laughter. To be the one who made her laugh and smile.

Her beautiful smiles that came easier these days. Smiles often directed at me. Smiles that could change my mood in the blink of an eye, brighten my world, and make my chest ache with a sensation that was unfamiliar, yet somehow so reassuring.

Our lives meshed so easily. She liked to cook—I liked to watch and help her. We enjoyed listening to music, the melodies filling the apartment all the time now. We watched movies, played card games she always cheated at. I was delighted to find out she enjoyed cribbage as much as I did. She was a good player and a sore loser, our tournaments lasting days with meticulous score-keeping. I enjoyed challenging her. She had her own way of challenging me.

Her bruises had healed over the past few weeks. Her shoulder no longer caused her pain. I wasn't as confident her emotional injuries had healed as well. She was still nervous at times, anxious about leaving the office alone, although she tried to hide it. When I was close, she relaxed. Oddly enough, she did the same thing for me. Nothing seemed as important when I walked in the door and saw her waiting. The worries and stress took a back seat to her warmth and presence. It was addictive.

"You're working tomorrow night?" she asked, turning in my arms.

I looked down at her, noticing the furrow between her eyes. "Yes."

"One of your 'off the books' jobs?"

At my nod, her frown deepened.

"What?"

"Somehow, these 'jobs' make me nervous. I don't know where you are, what you're doing, or who you're with. I can't relax until you walk in the door."

"Hey," I soothed, cupping her cheek. "It's just a privacy thing," I lied. "Standard, run-of-the-mill job, but for VIPs. It's part of the contracts, that's all. They like having me around."

The worry still showed on her face and in her eyes. The blue always dimmed when she worried. I had to admit it was odd having someone worry over me, but I rather liked it.

I kissed the end of her nose. "But I can't be effective if I'm starved the day before." I spun her in my arms. "Now start cooking, woman."

She muttered something, and I pressed my mouth to her ear. "After dinner, I'm going to show you who is really boss around here, Tally. Consider it dessert."

She whimpered.

I walked away chuckling, choosing a bottle of wine to have with dinner. I glanced over and met her gaze. Her frank, now bright, clear gaze. I winked.

She smiled.

I won.

It was late when I got home the next night. The team had done a raid earlier, and I ran ops from outside. It was successful, with another horrid operation brought down. Not as large-scale as some, but every single one we erased was a check mark on our side. They wouldn't have a chance to grow. To hurt kids and women—to rob them of their lives.

Tally was asleep on the sofa when I got in. I sat on

the coffee table beside her, watching her sleep. She was restless, her fingers clenching and unclenching on the blanket. Her head moved, her bright hair bunching around her face. She was frowning in her sleep— another sign of her anxiety. She was worried about me. Sometimes I thought she knew there was more to what I did than I told her. That, deep down, she suspected but was waiting for me to tell her. And I would soon. We'd found out more intel on her brother and his gang, and none of it was good. He was headed in the exact direction that would make him a target for Hidden Justice. If he had been the good boy Tally thought he was, the man he had grown into was nothing but a twisted shell. I was convinced she would never be completely safe until he was truly gone. And I was determined she be safe. Safe to live a life, free and open —with me.

I had learned so much about her the past while. She was a morning person, out of bed early, ready to face the day, but by ten, she was sleepy and cuddly, looking for the comfort of our bed—and me. She wasn't big on meat, but she had never met a bread she didn't love. Toast, the kind with a crispy crust and dripping with butter, was her favorite breakfast or snack. When she informed me mournfully it was the cause of her wide hips, I carried her to our room and showed her exactly how I felt about those hips.

Three times.

I thrilled at every new habit, nuance, or impulse I discovered about her. I luxuriated in the time we spent alone, enjoyed showing her the things I was passionate about, and loved every moment we shared.

I loved *her*. The words were as simple as they were complex. It had hit me one day when I realized she'd been with me for two weeks and I had caught her mutterings about being time to get back to reality and having a place she had to get back to. I didn't want her to go. Not in two weeks—not ever. The thought of not seeing her every evening, not having her warm body wrapped around mine at night, was unacceptable. The thought of her being alone again made me anxious. The thought of being without her made my chest ache. She filled my apartment with life. She filled my life with brightness.

Yet, I hadn't been able to tell her. Say the words. They didn't come easily to me. My mother had died when I was a kid, and my father was never demonstrative. He was a hardworking man and was never unkind, but also stoic and quiet a great deal of the time. There were no hugs, no feelings ever expressed. We had no other family, so I grew up surrounded by silence. Even with friends in later years, I found it difficult to articulate personal, deep emotions. It was somewhat easier with Tally, but it didn't come naturally for me the way it seemed to for her.

On the other hand, anger and rage were easy for me. Disgust, revenge, and rancor not an issue. I had zero guilt when it came to killing the men and women who perpetrated crimes against other humans. The truly evil ones with no conscience or remorse and who would continue to wreak havoc if not eliminated. That was the basis of Hidden Justice. We wiped the earth of them, not allowing the judicial system to fail as it often did. Governments and law agencies overlooked our work, knowing what a service we provided to humankind. Officials refused to acknowledge our existence and turned a blind eye to our methods. It worked well for all of us.

But with Tally, I was experiencing different emotions. I wanted to care for her, make sure she was all right. I wanted to hold her when she was sad, comfort her when she was upset. Share in her joy. Share in her life.

I didn't want to lose her. I *couldn't* lose her. The thought of going back to the constant gray my life was before she entered it was abhorrent. She brought out so many colors I had never seen before. And she did it all by simply being her.

I reached out, running my hand over her wild curls, and cupped her face. She woke, her blue eyes soft with slumber. She smiled, covering my hand with hers and pressing it into her cheek.

"Hi," she mumbled, her voice raspy from sleep.

"Hi," I replied, bending to kiss her.

"How was it?" she asked anxiously.

"Smooth and successful. Everything is good, baby."

"Are you hungry?"

I shook my head, spinning a curl around my finger. "Not for food."

"Oh." Her eyes went round, and she bit the corner of her lip. "I see."

I grinned. "I want a shower and to hold you in our bed."

She sat up, pushing back the hair from her face. I noticed a cut on her hand, and I caught it, studying the angry-looking mark.

"What happened?"

"Oh, when I was giving my place a clean, I knocked a glass I had off the shelf. I cut myself cleaning it up."

"Your place?" I questioned, feeling a knot in my stomach.

"Yes."

"Why were you at your old place?"

"Getting it ready." At my horrified gaze, she shook her head. "I'm fine now, Julian. All healed. And not being at the bar, no one is looking for me. It's time for me to go back to—"

I cut her off. "No," I stated firmly.

"Excuse me?" she replied, her voice cool.

"You can't." I grabbed her hands before she started swinging. I brought them to my mouth, kissing them, letting my mouth ghost over the mark on her skin. "Don't ask me to take you back there. I can't."

"Why?' she asked, her voice trembling.

"I want you here, with me."

Her anger bled through her words. "Because *why*? You like to fuck me? Have your dinners made? Your apartment clean? Someone to play cribbage with? Why do you want me to stay, Julian?"

I dropped to my knees in front of her, my heart racing in my chest. "Yes, all of those things. But most importantly, because I love you."

Shock registered on her face. "What?" she whispered.

"I love you, Taliyah Wells. I want you here with me. Always. Don't go back to a place where I can't protect you. Don't leave me alone here."

"Julian." Her voice was low, surprised.

"Stay."

"But—"

"Marry me."

TALLY

I was stunned into silence. First, by Julian's declaration of love—a sentiment I knew he found hard to express. He showed me all the time with his gestures, the way he cared and looked after me. With his body repeatedly, his murmurs and words of passion sinking into my skin, branding me as his.

But his asking me to marry him? That took me completely by surprise.

I met his gaze. His unwavering, intense gaze. I couldn't doubt his sincerity. It blazed from his stare, his focus entirely on me.

He was always watching me. Observing, noticing, his gaze taking in tiny details nobody else would even perceive. Every time I looked up when he was around, I knew I would be met with his return stare. I also knew he watched me from his desk. I had discovered the small camera while tidying the office. I pretended I didn't notice it, or the others like it around, but given what he did for a living, I wasn't surprised, and now I knew what he used the second monitor on his desk for. From the dust around them, I knew they'd been there a long time, not something he'd put in after I was hired. But I had no doubt he watched me some days. It should creep me out. I should demand the removal of the cameras.

But somehow, knowing how carefully he watched me, understanding that this need to protect me drove him somehow, only left me with a feeling of ease. I was safe. Always safe here, with him.

And I had fallen for him—hard. His intensity didn't frighten me. His bossiness and the certainty of his decisions were sexy. He didn't apologize or mince words. He ran a tight ship and had the respect of the men he oversaw. He was commanding and confident. I liked that part of him.

I got to see a different side to him. Funny, teasing, and even when the words were edged with arrogance, he was charming. He hid his softer side from the world, only showing the in-control man he had to be. He showed me that part of him, his touches tender, his voice low and caring. He expressed his thoughts out loud about how much he liked having me there with him. He praised my cooking, watched stupid shows on TV I knew he had no desire to view, yet he did it because he knew I wanted to. I loved the way he challenged me. I adored our silly but epic cribbage battles that went on without end, neither of us ready to give in. I loved the fact that he gave as good as he got and didn't let the fact that I was a woman come into play. He was as determined to win as I was. I loved to hear his laughter, to be the one to make him laugh. He seemed to enjoy our alone time as much as I did.

He was content—I would even say happy—when we were together, nothing and no one in the world but us.

Before I came along, I had the feeling he spent too much time alone. Too much time thinking, working, living moment to moment with no plans for the future.

It would seem he had been planning a future. With me.

I swallowed around the dryness in my throat. His hands tightened on mine.

"Julian," I murmured. "Don't be ridiculous. You're simply reacting. You don't want to marry me."

"Reacting?" he replied, his tone calm.

"To my leaving. We'll see each other every day at the office."

"First off, I'm not reacting, and second, every day isn't enough. I want you all the time." He cocked his head. "Do you not feel the same way about me, Tally?" He dropped his voice. "You said so last night, in your sleep. You whispered you loved me. It made me smile to hear those words."

I blinked.

I had said that?

I sighed, unable to withhold those words from him. "I do love you, Julian. So very much. So much, in fact, it frightens me."

"Don't let it frighten you. I assure you I return your sentiments tenfold." He held my hands to his chest. "I love you, Tally. And I want to marry you. I want to build a life with you."

"Has anyone ever mentioned you go from zero to sixty in five seconds?"

He grinned. "Three seconds, usually."

"You tell me you love me and want to marry me at the same time, and you wonder why I'm hesitant?"

"You think it's because you just told me you're moving back to your old place? That I'm reacting?"

"Pretty coincidental."

He slid his hand into his pocket, holding out a small box. "Not reacting, Tally. I already knew what I wanted."

I gazed at the box, too overwhelmed to reach out and take it. Too frightened to believe this was real and he wanted me as much as I wanted him.

He pressed the box into my hand and opened the lid. Inside, a pretty ring glowed against the satin, the sapphires and diamonds twinkling in the light. It was lovely, unique, and special.

"I love your eyes, and I wanted to signify that," he explained. "I saw this in an antique shop window, and I knew it was meant to be yours." He held it up. "I want to put this on your finger and hear you say I do."

He paused, waiting for my reply. "Tell me yes, baby. Marry me."

I couldn't deny him. I didn't want to deny him. "Yes."

CHAPTER TEN

Julian

T ally was in my arms, our bodies melded together. I nuzzled her head, then asked a question I was certain I already knew the answer to.

"Do you want a big, fancy wedding?"

"No," she scoffed. "For whom? The guys at Elite?"

I chuckled. "Would you agree to a small, quick wedding?"

She paused. "How quick?"

"We fly to Vegas this weekend, get married, and I'll take you on a honeymoon in a couple weeks."

"Julian," she said, aghast.

"What? I know what I want. So do you. Why should we wait?"

She lifted her head, peering at me. "You know, when I first met you, I thought you were probably the most cautious man I had ever met."

"I am. Unless it comes to you."

"What's the hurry?"

"I want to take you away. As my wife. I have a

couple of commitments to meet, and then we can go. A license here takes weeks."

"Go away?"

I drew in a deep breath. "I have a friend who owns a place in the Mediterranean. It's private. Peaceful. He and his wife have invited us to visit."

I planned on telling her everything there. About Hidden Justice. The truth about her brother. Let her absorb it all and come to terms with it. Then we could move forward with our life together with no more secrets.

She hesitated.

"You have a passport, right?"

"Yes."

"You love me and want to marry me?"

"Yes."

"I need one more yes, Tally. Do this with me. We're both alone, and we don't have to be. Take my last name and be my family. We'll make our own together."

"You want kids?"

"I want everything with you."

"Can I finish my degree?"

"Yes."

"And work toward my dream?"

"Yes."

"What if…" She trailed off, and I knew what her worry was.

"You don't have to hide anymore, baby. Not with me by your side. I promise you will be safe."

She cupped my face. "Then you get your third yes."

I kissed her, showing her everything with my touch and lips I couldn't say out loud.

How precious she was. How much she meant to me. How I would protect her with my life.

In time, she would understand it.

Tally wasn't happy when I told her I was doing a job out of town. She settled her hands on her hips, tapping her fingers impatiently.

"And if I forbid it?" she challenged, lifting her chin.

I chuckled and leaned down, kissing her pursed lips. "We took obey out of our vows, baby. For both of us. I don't want to be away from you, but it's in Quebec, it will be late, and it's easier to grab a hotel room and come home rested the next day."

"Don't throw our wedding vows at me."

I tilted my head. "You were so beautiful."

We'd jetted off to Vegas, got married, spent the night, and came home the next day. I had tried to make it romantic for her. She wore a pretty blue dress, and I donned a dark gray suit. I made sure she had flowers, got spoiled at a spa before the service, and her wedding band fit perfectly. When she had walked into the room, looking nervous, I'd lifted her hand to my mouth and pressed a kiss to it.

"You are the most beautiful bride ever," I promised her. "I'm the luckiest man in the world today."

"I feel the same about you," she replied, straightening my tie. "You always look so good in a suit."

I crooked my arm. "Shall we?" I winked. "The honeymoon can start right away."

"Let's go, then," she said with a laugh.

The ceremony was simple, fast, and perfect. The night we spent celebrating it was long, loud, and intense. We both slept on the plane on the trip home. I carried her over the threshold of the condo when we arrived. She laughed and cupped my cheek.

"I love you," she murmured.

It was one of the happiest days of my life.

She was now my wife and, therefore, protected in many ways. Ways she never thought of. She was the beneficiary of my will, my life insurance, and on record at Hidden Justice as my spouse. If anything untoward happened, she would be contacted and looked after. It gave me great peace of mind.

But tomorrow, I was going after her brother. Damien and I were meeting with the team there in the morning, finalizing all the strategies, and moving in that night. They'd scheduled a meeting of the top members. Dean was intent on moving into the next level of crime. That included illegal weapons and underage prostitution. Pornography. He was no longer satisfied with small-time crime. He wanted the big money, and he didn't care who he hurt to get it. Listening to the conversations, watching the videos, I'd been ill at the level of coldness he portrayed. Every bug and camera we'd managed to plant showed how far off the deep end he had gone.

His plans and his gang were going to end now.

"Stop it," Tally said, smacking my chest and

bringing me out of my thoughts. "You're trying to distract me."

"It's only one night, Tally." I had told them I was stepping back from the missions. The feeling that I was running out of time had taken hold, and I needed to heed that sensation. I had Tally now, and she was more important. I would work behind the desk now the way I had intended until the day I walked away entirely.

"You've been so busy," she said, worrying her lip. "I feel as if you're gone all the time."

I had been away frequently since we got married. I knew I'd been preoccupied and living in my head a lot. Making up pretend meetings, overnight trips, wanting to be sure we had everything nailed down. This mission —*she*—was too important to me to leave anything to chance. I would make it up to her once this was over.

"It's the last one for a long time."

"Promise?"

"Yes. You stay home tomorrow and be here when I get back the next day. Relax. Go get a massage or something. You look a little tired, so you should pamper yourself. When I get home, we'll plan our trip."

I had video-called Matteo, telling him I was married. He got Evie on-screen with him, and she had spoken to Tally, excited and filled with happiness for us.

"You'll have such a good time here, you'll never want to leave," she had exclaimed. *"It's so beautiful and peaceful!"*

"I look forward to meeting you," Tally assured her. *"Julian has such lovely things to say about you."*

"Give Matteo your contact info, and I'll be in touch."

I nodded at Tally. I knew I could trust Evie.

"Okay," she replied. "I look forward to it."

She slipped from my lap and left the room, and I turned back to the screen, meeting Matteo's amused expression.

"Missy and Marcus will be delighted as well," Matteo stated. "Marcus won the bet."

I lifted an eyebrow at Matteo. "You bet on me getting married?"

He chuckled, his gaze focused on Evie as she left the room. "He called it. He said you were more like me than he was and you wouldn't wait."

"I waited a few weeks, unlike you. You married Evie in a few hours."

He shrugged. "Best decision of my life. And I know yours will be as well. Finish your business and come here. That will be your second smartest decision." He paused. "And, Julian?"

I waited.

"Be honest with her. Nothing destroys love more than loss of trust."

"I am. I'm going to tell her everything once this is done. Then we'll figure out our future."

"Good."

He clicked off, and I shut down my laptop. I ran a hand over my face, feeling weary. I wanted this finished and over. I wanted to tell Tally and move forward. Build our life together.

I stood and went to find her.

Soon, we could start.

Rain beat down, the rhythmic sound not helping with my already stretched nerves. It added another layer of complexity to what we were going into. Entering a strange building, locking it down, capturing the people inside, destroying whatever criminal endeavors they were creating within the walls. I glanced over at Egan and Damien. I had called in a favor and got Egan back for this job. He had worked with Marcus and was the best demolition man I knew. Once we were done, I wanted the building razed. Although we didn't make a habit of taking out biker gangs, if any of them were thinking of expanding into the darker side of the law, this would send a message.

They were both calm and focused. The entire crew was. Outwardly, I was the same, but inside, I was a mass of emotions. I had never partaken of a mission that had personal involvement. Anger at Tally's brother, outrage at what he had put her through for nothing, the fact that I was going to have to tell her the truth and watch her heart break all over again added to the fire. And for the first time ever, I experienced a feeling of worry. My mortality had never bothered me before. I'd had nothing to lose. Now everything was wrapped around a sassy redhead who owned me, body and soul. It was disconcerting.

"On my mark," I murmured. Everyone was ready, everyone in position. We would converge, leaving no room for those inside to run.

Then it was go time.

The takedown was swift and efficient. They weren't expecting us. Dean's arrogance that he was above everything and everybody became clear, given the ease with which we broke in to their headquarters. Drugs, guns, girls. It was all there. The men knew exactly what to do, separating the ones we'd identified as the top officials to one space. One crew looked after the women who were sobbing in relief at being freed. Others packed up the guns and drugs, not chancing them falling into anyone else's hands.

I hunted down Dean. Like all cowards, as soon as he realized he was caught, he'd slunk away, hoping to escape, not caring about the fate of anyone else. He didn't blink an eye at the fallen bodies of his team as our guns took them out when they began firing our way. He turned and ran.

I followed dark hallways, already certain of the direction he was heading. A hidden back entrance that opened to the woods behind the building. I was sure he thought that he would lie low until we were gone and then reappear, collecting hidden monies and drugs and move on to start again. He had no idea the building would be blown up.

Or that I wouldn't let him escape.

I paused outside the room where the hidden door was located. Inside, I could hear movement, low and hurried. Mumbled curses. I glanced at the floor, noting the spots of blood. He'd already been hit. Unease skittered along my spine, anxiety making me tighten the grip on my gun.

"Damien," I murmured low into my mouthpiece. "Backup, rear left quadrant."

I slipped inside, the low light showing me he was across the room, pulling money from a safe. The back of his jacket shone bright with blood.

"Stop what you're doing, Dean. Hands up and turn around."

He froze, then slowly raised his hands. He turned and met my gaze, his baleful and angry.

"I can make this worth your while," he offered. "Lots of cash. You just turn your back for a moment, and I'll be gone."

I barked out a laugh, advancing toward him. He moved away from the safe, and we circled each other like animals getting ready for a fight. "I turn my back and you shoot me, you mean."

He shrugged. "Like you wouldn't do the same." He moved, sliding more to the right, and I followed, my gun trained on him.

The lights flickered, my apprehension growing. "You can't run. It's over, Dean. All of it."

"I don't think so."

"Running and hiding—that's what you do, isn't it? Like a coward. You lie, steal, intimidate, and take."

He flashed a grin. It was cold and menacing. "We all have our talents." He slid to the right again.

"Even with family?" I asked, matching him step for step. I wanted him to know this was personal.

"I have no family."

I said one word. "Taliyah."

His eyebrows rose. "That stupid little bitch again? I thought I got rid of her. I should have drowned that weak kitten while I had the chance." He shook his head. "That fucking troublemaker. First, she shows up and takes the attention from me yet again, then she almost takes part of my inheritance. I had worked the old lady

144

far too long for that. Hoodwinked her. She had no idea how much that fucking land was worth. I should have killed Taliyah instead of putting the fear of God into her." He snorted. "Not that it was difficult." His dislike was evident in his voice, his hatred bleeding through. It would break Tally's heart.

Anger built inside me. "That 'weak kitten' pushed on despite being scared and made a life for herself. She is *anything* but weak. Her biggest mistake was trusting, loving, the man she thought of as her brother."

He shrugged, clearly not caring. "I only put up with her for my grandmother's sake. She held the keys to my fortune, so I played along." Then he narrowed his eyes. "What is Taliyah to you?"

"My wife," I snarled. "And now under my protection. You'll never get a chance to hurt her again."

He laughed. "How droll. The little bitch married a narc and cried the blues, so you came to bust me. What a joke."

He stopped moving, and I aimed my gun. "Not a narc, asshole. I'm your worst nightmare. You won't see dawn or any of your drugs or fortune again. I'll make sure she gets it."

His rage filled the room, feeding the already heavy atmosphere.

An evil, twisted grin curled his mouth, his eyes practically glowing. "I'm going to watch you die and enjoy it. Then I'm going to go after your wife and kill her slowly. Or maybe I'll follow through with my threat and give her to a gang to enjoy. She'll wish for death by the time they're done with her."

The anger became fury, obliterating everything in its course. "You fucking piece of shit." I cocked my gun, any thoughts of leniency gone. "You better prepare to say hello to the devil. I hope you rot in hell."

There was a sound behind me, and a violent, red-hot pain tore through the top of my left pec, the burning and tearing of my flesh knocking me forward. The room wavered around me, and I struggled to stay upright. I glanced down at the bullet hole just as another gunshot rang out and tore through my bicep. Agony twisted my gut as I spun, shooting blindly. A woman screamed, slumping to the floor, the gun in her hand landing on the cement. Dean had lured me into the perfect spot for the hidden woman to shoot me, and I had let him. I had let my personal anger override my training and thoughts. She twitched, and I shot her again, not taking any chances.

There was a roar from Dean, and I was tackled from behind. We went down hard, and my fight-or-die impulse kicked in. We rolled, both bleeding, throwing punches, grabbing at flesh, cursing and tearing, desperately trying to find purchase on the other. Black spots flashed around me as I pushed against Dean, but he punched hard at my bullet wound, the pain so intense I groaned, my body weakening for a moment, giving him the advantage. He loomed over me, his face twisted into a smile so evil I felt nauseous. I needed to give Damien more time to get here—to find me.

"Any last words, loser?" he snarled.

"You won't make it out of here alive."

He laughed. "I beg to differ." He pressed his gun to

my head. "I hope that little bitch has good widow's benefits. Somehow, I'll get my hands on those too." He sneered. "Maybe I'll play the tragic big brother who has been in hiding to protect her. It'll be sweet when I take it all in the end."

My wrath exploded, and with a snarl, I grabbed for his gun, and we wrestled, the gun going off, grazing his head. He cursed and punched me, my nose breaking under his fist. He wrenched the gun from my hand, pressing it to my head again.

My thoughts drifted, Tally at the forefront. Sadness filled my chest. I would never hold her, never get to tell her how much I loved her. Never see her grow round with our children or watch them grow up. I had wasted my chance, and now it was too late. Anxiety flooded me, knowing she would be at his mercy. I had failed.

He pressed harder, pinning me down. I shut my eyes, not wanting to see his face as I died. I wanted her face, her voice, to be the last thing I saw and heard. To see that smile one more time, even if it was only in my mind. The sound of a gun engaging echoed in the room, making my eyes fly open. Shock and agony registered on Dean's face, blood spilling across his chest, and he crumpled forward, falling on top of me. I groaned at his weight, grateful when Damien grabbed him, rolling him off me.

He knelt down, radioing for help. "Stay focused, Julian."

I grunted. "I'm trying."

He pressed down, trying to slow the blood loss.

"Right above the vest. Lucky shot. Stay with me. Help is on the way."

"Make sure Tally is okay. Promise me you'll watch out for her."

"Don't talk shit like that. You'll be fine."

Darkness edged in on my vision. "Promise me."

"I promise. But you're going to be around to do it yourself. And she is going to kick your ass over this."

I smiled as I drifted away. I would let her.

I woke up slowly, my body one massive ache. I let myself assess my injuries before I opened my eyes. My shoulder and chest burned with the fire of a thousand suns. My arm wasn't far behind it. My face felt swollen, and the rest of me felt as if a Mack truck had run over me a few times.

Images, fractured and disjointed, ran through my head. The rain, the dark building, running, gunshots. Dean towering over me. Damien taking him out. Fading away.

Other memories filtered through. Soft hands, a gentle voice, my name being sobbed.

Tally.

My eyes flew open, the room coming into focus. She was standing to the side, staring out the window, her arms wrapped around her waist. I spoke her name, the word raspy and low. She turned, our eyes meeting. She looked exhausted and worn. Defeated and sad. I held out my hand, shocked to see how it shook. She slipped her hand into mine, holding it loosely.

"Am I dreaming?"

"No."

"Where am I?"

"Toronto General."

"How?"

"Once you were stabilized, you were airlifted here."

I swallowed, my throat dry. "How much—"

She cut me off. "I know everything. Damien told me."

I shut my eyes at the blatant hurt and anger in her voice.

"Not his place," I objected.

"Don't you dare," she hissed. "We didn't know if you would make it. I needed to understand why you were so injured. What the hell you'd been doing. Exactly what you'd been hiding from me." Her eyes flashed. "I should have heard it from you."

"I was trying to protect you."

"Me, or yourself?" she shot back.

I wasn't sure how to respond.

"Damien wanted me to know how many people you helped save. How you always put Hidden Justice first. That you were highly regarded by your men and the organization." A sob caught in her throat. "And how determined you were to make sure I was safe from the terrible person my brother had become. Damien wanted me to know who you really were—that the man I married was more than I knew." She shook her head. "It should have been you telling me, Julian. You should have given me the choice if you went after Dean or not."

Her voice caught. "All the times you walked out the door without saying you loved me. The conversations you avoided. The distance I felt between us. I thought you regretted marrying me."

"No," I rasped. "I was trying to make you safe. I was so wrapped up in my head, Tally. I kept thinking you'd understand when I told you. I didn't mean to make you think—" I swallowed. "I never thought—"

The doctor walked in, and she moved away, letting go of my hand. I felt the loss of her touch immediately. I had a feeling it would be a while until I felt it again.

For two days, I was in and out. When I woke, Tally was there, an ever-present shadow. She rarely spoke, her touches only given to help, never to bridge the gap I felt between us. On the third day, I was more alert, the fog disappearing. The doctor declared me on the road to recovery.

"We'll keep you another few days, then send you home to heal."

Tally helped me to shower and change into fresh clothing. Made sure I ate. Smiled at Damien, Egan, all the men who came to see me. Sat quietly, making sure I didn't overdo it. Yet barely a word passed her lips, and each moment, she looked more exhausted, and I felt her slip further away from me.

At the end of the day, she helped me settle, and I noticed her purse on the chair.

"Going somewhere?" I asked, my voice tight.

"I need a change of clothes and some sleep," she said.

"Are you coming back?"

She stared at me, silent, and I reached for her hand. "Forgive me. Give me a chance to explain, Tally. We can work this out."

She bent, cupping my face, our eyes locked. I saw the worry and hurt. The hidden fear deep in her eyes. She kissed me, her mouth moving with mine. I kissed her back, the feel of her lips on mine both perfect and wrong at the same time. I gripped her arms, keeping her close. Sadness welled at the feeling of losing something that was slipping away. Losing her. I kept kissing her.

I tasted her pain and anger. Her desperation. She pulled away, staring down at me, still silent. She picked up her purse and left.

It wasn't until later when I was alone, I realized I had tasted her goodbye.

PRESENT DAY

CHAPTER ELEVEN

Tally

I shifted in the uncomfortable seat in the airport, uneasy and tense. I looked up at the departure board, but the status of the flight I was waiting on remained unchanged. I heard the mutterings of other passengers—mechanical issues, a problem on the runway, all various thoughts on why our flight was delayed.

I inhaled a calming breath, scanning the small waiting area. Nothing seemed out of place. People milled about, bored and wanting to leave. One older couple sat across from me, never moving. She read a book while he did crosswords, occasionally asking her a question. They were obviously at ease and not worried about the delay, taking it in stride. She had cooed over Julianna, her husband barely looking, but other than that, seemed to forget I was there. No one was looking at me, nothing was amiss, yet I was on high alert. I thought I had it all mapped out—every last detail. I had stuck to the plan the entire time I had been here. I was certain no one had ever been as meticulous about a three-day trip as I had been. A trip I had dreaded and looked forward to at the same time. One I had to make since time was no longer on my side. I had owed it to her.

I exhaled and glanced down at the small bundle in my arms. My daughter's eyes gazed up at me, wide and alert, the colors vivid in contrast to her pale skin. Curls, so adorable and wild in a darker shade of red than mine, lay against her head. Her fist was in her mouth, a sure sign she was hungry. We should have been on the flight by now. I would have fed her, and she would have slept. She was so good about sticking to her schedule, flying or not. I was extremely lucky that way. I glanced around, the closest restroom small and not accommodating to sit and feed her in private.

I stood and approached the desk where a woman was tapping out something on her keyboard. She looked up as I approached, offering me a resigned smile, no doubt certain I was about to quiz her on the situation. I offered a smile in return.

"Is there a family restroom close by?" I asked. "Someone is hungry, and it's so crowded over there."

"Oh," she replied with a nod. "There is."

Another woman appeared, interrupting. "It's closed at the moment. But come with me. There is a small private room down the hall you can sit in and feed your child."

Julianna squirmed in my arms, making a whimpering noise.

"She heard the word feed." I laughed.

The woman, who introduced herself as Shannon,

took my bag, and I followed her down a short hall. In the sparse room were a table and chairs, plus two loungers. A window high up let in the last afternoon sun. "This will be more comfortable for you. In fact, feel free to stay here until the flight is called. As soon as it's ready to board, I'll come get you."

I felt a rush of gratitude. It was cooler and quiet in here. Private. I relaxed a little. "That would be lovely."

"Water?" she asked. "I know you have to keep hydrated."

"Thank you."

A few minutes later, Shannon returned with a bottle of water and left. "I'll be back to check on you."

"Any idea when the flight will be ready?"

"I heard about an hour or two at the most. The part is set to arrive any minute."

Grateful for the update, I sat in one of the loungers, settling Jules at my breast, smiling as she latched on fast. I stroked her plump cheek softly, watching as her eyes shut as she fed. She was a good eater. A good baby. I felt a rush of guilt that I tamped down as I watched her. She looked so much like Julian. Her eyes, the shape of her mouth. The dimple high on her cheek that he had which only came out when he smiled a certain way. She was a constant reminder of what I had lost. Of what I missed so much on a daily basis.

I stroked over her hair, humming low, relaxing. Soon, we'd be in the air, and I would get back to my life. Or, at least, the life I was attempting to make. The truth was, I was lost. Lost without *him*. But I had made a choice and put my daughter first. She was what mattered—the most important thing in all of this.

She finished feeding, and I burped her, changed her, then sat down, holding her close. The room was quiet, the sounds from the terminal muffled. It was a good thing Shannon would be coming to get me as I couldn't hear any boarding announcements or updates in here. I caught the occasional sound of footsteps as people passed the door and low conversations in the hall, but no one entered. I glanced at the clock, wondering if Shannon would return soon. It had been about an hour, so I expected an update at least.

An odd feeling prickled under my skin, and I tried to ignore it. I felt an awareness, a tugging in my chest. I stood and paced the room, stopping to open the door and peek out. No one was there, and the sounds of the bustling airport were all I heard. I shut the door and shook my head as I transferred Jules to my other arm. I was being paranoid. I had been the whole trip, and now I was simply anxious to get through the final stage and return to hiding. That was all, I assured myself.

Until I heard the sounds of heavy, measured footsteps approaching and stopping at the door. There was a beat of silence, a pause, then a knock—deviously light and quiet, yet somehow screaming loud in my head. I watched as the handle turned, and the door opened.

Julian entered the room, our eyes clashing across the small space. For a second, my breath stopped, the power of the moment overwhelming me. He was every bit as tall and handsome as I remembered. His shoulders were broad and set back, and his countenance intense. He was thinner than I recalled, the lines around his eyes more pronounced, and his anger was palpable. Fury drew down his eyebrows and pulled at his mouth. His gaze was focused, first on my face, then the small bundle I held tight in my arms.

All my planning, all my careful maneuvering, was for nothing. It was time to face what I had run away from.

I lifted my chin.

"Hello, Julian."

JULIAN

She was beautiful. Even more so than my memory or the pictures I had of her let me think. She stood across from me, brave and defiant, the lie she perpetuated asleep in her arms.

My daughter.

I was hungry for a look. I wanted to hold her. I wanted to hold her mother. But anger colored my feelings, and I narrowed my eyes. "Taliyah."

Silence stretched until I stepped forward. She moved back, holding out her hand as if to ward me off.

"How did you find me?"

"One of my men spotted you. He was waiting for the same flight."

"Which one?"

"The older man seated across from you."

She frowned. "He barely looked at us."

I shrugged. "He let you think that. He was watching you closely. He called me."

"My flight—"

"Has departed."

She gaped at me. "What?"

"Your luggage was taken off. It's waiting for you outside in the car."

"How dare you," she hissed, keeping her voice low.

I stepped closer, towering over her. "How dare I? *How dare I?* You disappear, hiding for over a year, keeping my child from me, and you ask me How. I. Dare?"

"She's not yours," she lied.

I laughed without humor. "You still can't lie for shit, Tally. You expect me to believe you ran off, had an affair and another man's child right away, given the passion we shared? The love we felt for each other?" I shook my head. "I'm not an idiot."

"Maybe I had the affair while we were together."

"I can't believe you would even say that. You know as well as I do there was no one but each other for us."

A flush saturated her cheeks, but she didn't deny it.

"Let me see her."

"No."

I held out my arms. "Let me see my daughter, Tally. Now." My tone brooked no argument.

Tears filled her eyes, and her body shook.

"I'm not going to hurt her."

"But you're going to take her away," she whispered, fear tearing at her words.

I felt her pain as if it was my own. It had been like

that since we had started. I softened my voice. "No, I'm not. I want to meet her."

Tears ran unheeded down her pale cheeks as she placed our daughter into my arms. For a moment, the world stopped as I gazed into her tiny face. Took in the plump cheeks, downy red curls, and the pursed rosebud lips. Emotions I had never experienced until now thundered inside me. Joy, alive and bubbling, hit my chest. Love, so deep and unexpected, swelled for the tiny being in my arms. Rage that she had been hidden from me, that I might never have known her existence, bubbled and burned.

Then she opened her eyes, and I was shocked into awareness. I was holding my daughter. My flesh and blood. My eyes were reflected back at me, crystal clear evidence of her parentage, staring, curious and confused. I stroked along her cheek with my finger, a thrill running through me as she grasped the digit, holding on fast.

"Her name?" I managed to get out.

"Julianna Grace."

I snapped my head up, meeting Tally's eyes.

"I call her Jules," she added.

"She is…amazing," I said, unable to form the right words.

"Please don't take her from me, Julian. Please." A sob broke her voice. "I couldn't bear it."

I frowned as I looked at Tally. Our time apart had changed her, letting me know it hadn't been easy on her either. She was too thin, too exhausted, and too far away. Even in my anger, I still loved her. That was an absolute fact that would never change.

It also didn't explain why'd she left, why she came back, or why she'd hidden my daughter from me.

I wanted answers.

"I'm not going to take her away," I assured her. "But neither are you."

"We can arrange visitation. I won't keep her from you."

I narrowed my eyes. "There'll be no need for visitation, Tally. We'll be in the same home, so I can see her whenever I want."

She swallowed, her eyes large in her face. "What?"

"You heard me. You're coming home with me, and we're going to talk."

"My home is elsewhere."

I stepped closer, sliding my daughter, who had been watching us, her little mouth frowning, back into her mother's arms. "Your *home*, your place, is with *me*. Both of you."

I was close enough I could smell her. She had always smelled good—pretty and feminine. Now there was another layer to her scent. Our daughter had added to it. One I would have to get used to.

And I planned on getting used to it fast.

"You can't tell me what to do."

I lifted an eyebrow. "You forget the man you're married to, Tally. One call and I *can* have our daughter taken from you. Charged with kidnapping. Have you locked up." I was full of bullshit, but I was angry. Tally grew pale at my threats.

"Or you can come with me quietly, and we can settle this between us."

"Settle what, exactly?" she asked, her bravado making me want to kiss her and yell at her at the same time.

"Where we go from here. One way or another, I'm back in your life. How you play it will decide how your future unfolds. I suggest you choose wisely."

"You're a bastard," she whispered through tight lips.

"No, I'm a husband and a father. I'm fighting to keep my family. And I'm not going to fight fair this time. You erased those rules. Now you can live with the ones I set out."

I saw the fight drain from her eyes. Watched her shoulders slump. I had won—at least for now. It was all I needed to get her back to the apartment so I could figure this out.

"Fine," she whispered. "You win."

Strangely, I didn't feel any sense of victory at her words.

CHAPTER TWELVE

Tally

I felt his eyes on me in the car the entire ride into Toronto, yet every time I looked at him, his gaze was on Julianna. He sat across from us in a limo, Julianna safely strapped into a car seat beside me. The silence was making me jittery.

"How did you arrange for the car seat so quickly?"

"I have connections."

"The same connections that got my luggage off the airplane?"

He shrugged. "They're far-reaching when need be."

"How did you know which one?"

He finally tore his gaze off Julianna, meeting mine. "I knew your alias five minutes after I got the call. Your luggage was taken off the plane ten minutes after they showed you the private room. The loudspeaker in the room was disconnected before you walked into it. A guard was stationed in the hall in case you tried to leave," he said flatly with no emotion as if reciting a grocery list, not spinning his web of trapping me.

"Who are you?" I wondered out loud.

"I told you. I'm your husband. The father of our child. I wasn't letting you slip away again."

"The man I married ran a security firm."

"The man you married was more than that, and you knew it. You chose not to see it, and I was stupid enough to allow it." He leaned forward. "I lied to protect you, and I have regretted it every day. I hated how you discovered my lie, but what I hated most of all was that you ran before you let me explain. That you walked away as if what we shared meant nothing." The look in his eyes became frostier. "That you hid our daughter from me and only by chance did I find out about her."

"I was trying to protect her."

He cocked his head. "And I was trying to protect you."

Another uneasy silence fell between us. Julianna squirmed, kicking her feet, and Julian leaned forward, rubbing her tummy. "Is she okay?"

"Yes. She's just fussing a little. Her schedule is off."

"Julianna," he crooned. "Pretty little girl." He smiled, tickling her chin, which seemed to delight her. I was amazed since she never liked strangers. I supposed I shouldn't be surprised she liked Julian. I wondered if she sensed their connection even as distant as it was.

He wound one of her curls around his finger. "She has your hair," he mused.

"A little darker."

He looked up, his eyes all at once vulnerable and pleading. "Why did you name her Julianna?"

"I wanted her to have something of her father's," I

said honestly.

"Besides my DNA?" he asked, a smile tugging at his lips. "The eyes sort of give it away."

"So does the impatience at mealtime."

He bent close to her and whispered something to her I didn't catch. I watched the scenery go by, the sights becoming familiar as we got closer to Toronto.

There was so much I wanted to say, so many questions I had to ask, but I was aware there was a driver and this wasn't the time or place.

"Are you still in the same place?" I asked.

"Yes. For now."

"Oh?"

"We'll need a house. With a yard. She'll need a swing set."

"She's too young for that. And I'm not staying."

He ignored me.

"I got a crib and other items you need for her. They'll be in place when we arrive. Whatever else you need, we can get tomorrow."

"There is no—"

He cut me off, leaning close and gripping my chin. He held it firmly but not tight—he controlled the pressure so as not to hurt me. He stared into my eyes.

"You aren't going anywhere, Tally. Not without me. Whatever life you were living, whatever you left behind, is your past. You are my wife, and Julianna is my daughter. You are staying with me. Do you understand?" He released his hold on my chin, running his knuckles over my cheek and tucking a curl behind my ear the way he always used to.

"You can't force me," I protested, even as I tried not to luxuriate in the feel of his touch. I had missed it so much. I had missed him.

"It won't be force."

"You're forcing me now," I pointed out.

"You need persuasion. We need time to talk, to forgive, and move forward."

"What if I can't forgive?"

He lifted his eyebrows, his gaze serious. "Then I will fight you for our daughter. I have a feeling I know who would win."

I felt the blood drain from my face. He was right. I had nothing to fight with. And I had run away, keeping her birth a secret. My past wasn't great either, and I had no steady income. Nor did I have the contacts he did.

"You would take my daughter away from me?" I managed to get out.

"I would fight to keep you. Both of you."

I had to turn away before he saw how his words affected me.

He spoke, his voice weary. "I believe you have had your own secrets, Tally—Julianna being among them. I think it's time we both bared our souls and let the dust settle."

I didn't reply.

The apartment looked the exact same as it did the day I left. Nothing had been moved or changed. I was certain my coffee cup was still waiting for me beside the

Nespresso machine. Julian carried Julianna, her little face scrunched against his shoulder, his large hand splayed across her back and head. I followed in silence, the only noise the wheels of my suitcase I pulled behind me. He walked past the master bedroom and into the guest room.

The bed was pushed against the far wall, and a crib and changing table were set up along the wall closest to the door. On the bed was a pile of baby clothes—used but in perfect condition. There were diapers, blankets, even a cheerful mobile hanging over the freshly made bed. A Diaper Genie sat ready beside the changing table, and bottles of baby products were lined up.

I shook my head. "I can't believe the head of a dangerous organization has people who shop for baby stuff at the drop of a hat."

That earned me a chuckle. "Leo and his wife had this stuff. I had heard him telling Anne they were going to put it up for sale. I called him from the helicopter and made him a deal. A bunch of the guys went and picked it up and brought it here. Leo's wife helped set it up."

I remembered Leo fondly. He was a soft-spoken man who did some security work on occasion for Julian and ran the building for him. I recalled Julian saying he'd been hurt once on a job gone wrong, and it was Julian's responsibility to make sure Leo was taken care of.

"Who is Anne?"

"My new secretary." He flashed me a grin that almost made me laugh. "She's terrible."

"Does she knit?"

"Needlepoint."

"Ah. Well, that's what you get for hiring old ladies."

"I had the best," he declared. "Nowhere to go but down."

I ignored him.

"You shouldn't have gone to all this trouble." I took Julianna from his arms when she began to fuss, and he looked upset.

"She's hungry. I have to feed her," I explained, wanting him to know he hadn't done anything wrong for some reason.

"Right." For the first time, he looked unsure. "What can I do? I have no baby food. Leo's wife, Gwen, didn't say anything about baby food."

"She's still breastfeeding. I need some water if possible. And some privacy."

I was shocked to see his cheeks flush. "Right. Water. I can do that. I'll be right back."

He bolted, and I sat down on the chair in the corner, settling Julianna at my breast. I stared down at her, trying not to cry. It wasn't good for her when I got upset. I had to stay calm and figure this out.

I had no other choice. Julian made that very clear. I just had to figure out how we settled this. Losing my daughter wasn't an option.

Julian came in with a large glass of water and ice, the sides of the glass slick with condensation.

"I remembered you liked lots of ice."

"Thank you."

He paused, uncomfortable. He ran a hand through his hair, then rubbed the back of his neck, clearly unsure what to do next.

"So, I'm going to order dinner. Give you some time. I'll be in the living room."

I nodded, keeping my gaze focused on Julianna. Her eyes were closed, her little fist bunching and unbunching as she fed.

"Is she okay?" he asked, his voice concerned.

"She does that. Always has. I think she enjoys eating, and that's how she shows it."

"Okay. Good. So, I'll be out there…" He trailed off.

It occurred to me he was nervous. Unsure of his place here. Although his worry was touching, this was my time to bond with Julianna.

"Fine," I murmured, not looking up.

He paused at the doorway, and I felt his stare.

I didn't return it.

JULIAN

Jesus, she was so beautiful, sitting and nursing our child.

Our child.

The words echoed in my head over and again as I walked down the hall. I went to the kitchen and poured a shot of scotch, downing it in one mouthful. I shook my head at the fire in my throat and the way the alcohol warmed my chest.

I reached for the phone, called Carlos, and ordered pizza, then added salad, dessert, and a chicken fettuccine since I wasn't sure if pizza was something nursing mothers ate. I hung up and wandered to the window, looking out over the bustling city.

I had no clue about mothers, nursing or not. Babies either.

It had never occurred to me that Tally could have been pregnant when she left me. She had been on birth control, but obviously, it failed. Given how often we'd made love, it wasn't surprising she got knocked up. I paused with the glass partway to my lips. Was that why she'd run? Worried over my reaction? We had never discussed kids in a serious fashion.

Then I shook my head. There was more. Instinctually, I knew it, but I didn't know why. Not the whole picture.

I heard the soft cries of my daughter from down the hall, and I had to stop myself from running to find out why. The intense feeling of protectiveness I felt for her was shocking. It was even stronger than the ones I had felt for Tally. But these were twisted up with fear and love. A need to nurture and care for the tiny being who had suddenly appeared in my life.

I had no idea what to do with all the feelings.

The noise stopped, and I sighed. Tally knew what to do for her. Earlier, I had watched her for a short time on the hidden camera in the room she had sat in at the airport. Saw how she rocked and held Julianna, changed her, and moved her around with an ease I envied. I had no clue how to hold a baby. I had never done so before.

She was obviously a good mother. Loving and caring. Devoted.

I thought about the intense fear that crossed her face

when I threatened to use my power to take Julianna away from her. I shouldn't have done so, but I was angry. Furious with her that she'd kept her a secret from me, horrified at the thought that if Conrad hadn't seen her, I could have missed years, if not her entire life.

And God help me, I wanted those years.

The sound of running water and Tally's voice cooing drew me back down the hall. In the adjoining bathroom, Tally was hunched over the sink, Julianna kicking in happiness as she lay in the water.

"Who loves her bath?" Tally asked, ticking Julianna's tummy. "Who loves to splash Mommy?" I was fascinated watching them. I had always been transfixed by Tally, and with Julianna in the mix? I feared I was straight-up obsessed.

Tally looked up, meeting my eyes.

"She was a bit milky and still fussy. I thought a bath would help. She usually drifts off after one."

"You can order her a proper tub tonight. Plus whatever else you need."

She didn't argue, concentrating on Julianna.

"Your friend brought some nice products. The lavender bath will help soothe her." She laughed, holding up a facecloth. "I do need some smaller cloths. Yours are like a towel for her."

"Sure. You can get whatever you want or need. I ordered dinner too."

She lifted Julianna from the sink, laying her on a towel she had on the counter and quickly tapping her dry and swaddling her.

"Did you want to hold her while I get her diaper and

onesie?"

I nodded eagerly, letting Tally settle her into my arms. I grinned as one small hand fought its way out of the towel, flailing around. I slipped my finger into the fist, chuckling.

"Is Daddy's girl so strong?" I murmured. "Such a hard grip."

I met Tally's eyes, shocked to see the tears in them. I stepped forward. "What, Tally? What is it?"

She shook her head, seemingly unable to speak. Without thinking, I pulled her close, pushing her head to my chest, the way I had always done when she was upset. She accepted my embrace, her arms going around my waist. I caught our reflection in the mirror, her and me together, me holding our daughter.

A family.

My world, my brain whispered.

I held my daughter, insisting Tally eat her meal. She took a little chicken fettuccine and salad, but she mostly pushed it around her plate. She refused the wine I offered, saying it upset Julianna's tummy.

I made a mental note to procure a book on babies and nursing mothers. I needed more information.

"You need to eat more than that, Tally," I scolded. "I don't know much, but I do know you need to fuel your body. She must deplete you constantly."

She didn't reply.

"If you don't like it, I'll order something else."

"It's fine. I'm not hungry."

"Don't punish me by punishing her," I snapped.

Tears filled her eyes. "I would never do anything to hurt my daughter."

"Our daughter. Stop omitting me," I demanded.

As if sensing the tension in the air, Julianna began to cry. Her face became red, the sound of her distress triggering a reaction in me I had never experienced.

Helplessness.

Tally jumped up and took her from my arms, holding her close. "It's okay, Jules. Mommy has you. It was just a noise." She glared at me. "She isn't used to yelling. If you insist on this, can you try not to be such a jerk around my—" she shut her eyes "—*our* daughter?"

I stood, running my finger down Julianna's cheek. "I'm sorry, little one."

"I'm taking her to bed. It's been a long day."

"Your dinner…" I protested. "I wanted to talk. We need to settle this."

"We are not going to settle anything in one night, Julian. And we're certainly not going to settle it tonight while I'm stressed and she's upset."

With that, she turned and walked away, the muffled sound of Julianna's cries echoing in my head for hours.

Shame and guilt burned through me. I shouldn't be yelling—especially around Julianna. And I knew today had been as great a shock to her as it had to me. We both had to adjust.

I sighed as I put away the basically untouched dinner.

Tomorrow would be a better day.

CHAPTER THIRTEEN

Julian

I was up and dressed early, unsure what to do. I had to go into the office, at least for a little while. Maybe if I was out of the apartment, Tally would relax a little. Eat.

I found her in the living room, a cup of coffee beside her and Julianna on her lap. She was talking and playing with her quietly, doing something called "Patty-cake." The sound of Julianna's sweet baby giggles made me smile. I moved forward, wanting to be part of the joy.

Except Tally saw me and stopped.

"No," I protested. "Keep playing."

"I'm sorry if we disturbed you."

"No, it's fine. You didn't," I replied, my voice sharper than I intended. "I'm heading to work soon."

Tally didn't look surprised. "Of course you are," she said dryly. "Will you be gone all day?"

Something in her voice angered me. I leaned close, keeping my voice low.

"Not all day, and even if I were, there is a guard

outside. Plus one downstairs. If you think you can disappear again, think again, Tally. I know your alias now. There is nowhere you can go I can't find you."

She gasped quietly. "That's not what I meant."

I shook my head, not believing her. "The repercussions would be swift and great this time."

She stood, holding the baby against her like a talisman. "I have no doubt," she replied. "I feel your anger and mistrust, Julian. I get it." She began to walk away. "Have a nice day," she added sarcastically. "I know how important your *work* is to you."

The soft thud of her bedroom door sounded like an explosion in the apartment.

I sat at my desk, unable to concentrate. I was bogged down in anger, guilt, worry, and indecision. For the first time in a very long while, I didn't want to be here. I wanted to be where Tally was, where Julianna was. I wondered what they were doing. Napping? Playing?

What was Julianna's schedule? Would she settle? Would Tally see the laptop and the note I left telling her to order whatever she wanted and I would fill in the credit card information when I got home later?

Would she realize I didn't simply leave the credit card because I was afraid she would use it to book a flight somewhere and try to leave?

I let my head fall back. It was true. I was worried about her leaving. Trying to run. Somehow slipping past the guards and getting away. She was resourceful enough. She'd hidden from me for over a year. None of my searches showed even a hint of her. I rubbed my tired eyes and stared at the ceiling. I had barely slept, too alert to what was happening across the hall all night. I heard Tally get up when Julianna fussed. I heard her getting water, and I knew she was feeding her. I listened as she walked, softly humming, and talking our daughter back to sleep. The urge to go and offer to help had been strong, but I knew she didn't want either my help or my company.

And if I was being honest, I couldn't blame her.

My anger kept flaring, sharp words and meaningless threats falling from my mouth without thought. Except Tally didn't know they were meaningless. I had frightened her—really frightened her. I could see it in her eyes, feel it in the air around her when I appeared.

I had to change that, but I wasn't sure how. I blew out a long breath. It seemed as if I was repeating the same errors I had before she'd left me the first time. Showing the wrong emotions and sending her mixed signals. I rotated my arm, trying to ease the stiffness in my shoulder, ease the tension that had built in the injured muscle. It still ached, and holding the baby so much hadn't helped. I wouldn't stop that, though.

The door behind me opened and Damien walked in, Leo with him.

"Bad time?" Damien asked.

"No, come in."

I glanced at the monitor with a shake of my head. Anne was napping at her desk, her needlepoint falling to her lap as she dozed. Part of me was jealous, the other part resigned and too exhausted to bother being annoyed. I clicked off the camera.

"What's up?"

Damien and Leo exchanged a look. "We thought we'd check in on you after yesterday's, ah, *developments*," Leo said. "I hope everything we brought over was useful?"

"Yeah, it was great."

"Gwen wondered if you needed anything else?"

"I told Tally to order whatever she needed. I think we're okay."

There was silence, then Damien chuckled. "Holding your cards tight to your vest as usual, Julian. How are things—really?"

I looked at the two men I trusted. Both had become more than part of my team. Damien was my trusted right-hand, and I had come to know Leo well since he had returned to the fold, so to speak. Both were hard-working, honest men. They offered their loyalty and friendship easily.

"Shit," I replied.

Leo leaned back, a slight grimace crossing his face. The beating he had taken from Xavier Zander had left permanent damage to his knees and shoulders before Marcus and Missy had taken Zander out. The bastard had been an expert in inflicting pain and injury.

"How is your daughter?" he asked quietly.

A smile tugged on my lips. "Perfect. Adorable. Strong." Then I frowned. "A stranger."

"That will change. Give it time." He paused. "And Tally?"

The words were out before I could stop them. "She fucking hates me. Not that I blame her. I keep acting like an ass. Threatening things I don't mean, upsetting her."

Again, they exchanged a look. "You have every right to be angry, Julian," Leo said. "But maybe you better dial it back. Tally is nursing, and stress isn't good for the mother or baby."

"I'm worried she'll take off. I'm already so in love with Julianna, I can't believe it."

"And Tally?" he asked again.

"I still love her."

Damien shifted in his chair. "I can't offer much in the way of relationship advice," he said with a smirk. "But I do know anger isn't the best way to get a woman to trust you again."

"Maybe you should go talk to Dr. Easton. Get out some anger, and she can give you some pointers to help rein it in. Then you should go home, apologize, and talk to Tally," Leo said in his quiet way.

It was good advice, and I nodded in silent agreement. I met Leo's gaze. "I know nothing about babies. The noises and squeaks. How to change a diaper. Give her a bath. Do things to help Tally. She seems so at ease with her, and I feel as if I'll drop her at any given second."

Leo laughed. "You've had her in your life less than a day. You're overwhelmed and in shock. Of course Tally is comfortable. She carried her for nine months. Been the one looking after her twenty-four seven since she was born. You need to cut yourself some slack, ask Tally for guidance, and read a couple of books." He shook his head. "And get the hell out of here and spend some time with both of them. Reconnect. Engage as a father and husband, not an angry jerk."

"When did you get to be so smart?"

"Gwen helped me." He pulled out his phone. "I'll send you the links to a couple of great books."

Damien spoke up. "We have nothing the rest of the week, Julian. All the teams are accounted for, and the strikes happening aren't here. I can run point. We can reach you at home. I'll stay in the office and make sure Anne doesn't fall out of her chair during her naps and handle any calls. Go be with them." He lifted his eyebrows. "It's not as if you're being very productive anyway."

I flipped him the bird, and he laughed. But he was right. I could handle whatever was needed from the office at home. Tally knew about Hidden Justice now, so it wasn't as if I had to hide that from her any longer.

I could spend some time with Tally and Julianna. Clear the air and try to move forward. Figure out this mess. As Leo said, reconnect. Find our common ground. I smiled grimly to myself.

Julianna.

She was our common ground.

I would start there.

Our daughter and an apology.

TALLY

I walked the apartment endlessly, rocking Julianna, soothing her. It was so unusual for her to be so fussy, but I wasn't surprised. I was edgy and hadn't eaten well, and it was affecting her. Finally, she settled, and I put her in the crib, staring down at her. Even asleep, she looked like Julian, so there was no denying her parentage even though I had tried. He was right. I had always been a horrible liar, and that hadn't changed.

Everywhere I looked were memories. Of him. Of us. I felt as if I had traveled back in time to the day I left. When I peeked in the closet of the master bedroom, I found clothes I had left behind. Some of my toiletries in the drawers of the vanity. He hadn't changed anything or thrown my things away. I would have thought that would have been the first thing he would have done. I carried some items into the guest room and put them away, grateful he hadn't gotten rid of them. I had brought so little with me here since most of the room was needed for Julianna's items. Babies required a lot of stuff when traveling. I rubbed at my breasts, feeling the ache. I needed to pump them, but I hadn't brought the pump with me, so I needed to get one.

I sat down at the table by the laptop, looking at Julian's note.

Buy what you need.
I'll pay for the cart when I get home.
Groceries can be ordered through this app—Fill Your Cart. Credit

card online already, so fill the fridge and cupboards. They are sparse.

I wasn't surprised he didn't leave me his credit card. He didn't trust me. I didn't think he ever fully did, which had been part of the problem. And now I barely recognized him. Julian had always been in control. He rarely displayed his real emotions, unless you counted his desire. That, he shared with me in spades. Our love life had been intense and passionate. The few times I saw his anger, it had been directed toward others— usually those he felt were going to hurt me.

Now, it was directed at me. I sighed as I stared at the cup of coffee I had made and not even tasted. I didn't blame him for his anger, but it scared me. The thought of him taking away Julianna struck a fear in me that ran so deep it made me tremble. His threats and barbed innuendos sent me into a tailspin.

Then at moments, he was gentle. Like when he embraced me after Julianna's bath. The look on his face when he first held her. That was the Julian I remembered. The man I missed so much at times I ached with it. When I had watched him with her after her bath, the emotion of the moment had hit me. He had held me so tenderly, and I felt such relief at being back in his arms, it scared me. I couldn't get used to that again.

I stared at the computer and made a decision. I opened the grocery app and filled the cart with everything I could think of. I needed to keep up my strength and eat properly for Julianna's sake. Then I clicked on Amazon, logging in to my old account, surprised somehow that it was still there and accepted the password I remembered. I went to the baby section and began shopping. Julian said to buy what I wanted or needed for both Julianna and myself.

I was going to do just that.

The door opened a short time later, and I looked up, surprised to see Julian home so soon. It had only been a few hours. The Julian I had known had a hard time tearing himself away from his office.

"Hello," I said warily.

"Hi," he replied, putting a bag on the table where I was sitting. He indicated the laptop. "Shopping?"

"Yes. I ordered groceries which should be here soon, and I have a full cart on Amazon. A very full cart."

He sat down, pulling the laptop close and looking at the items. Then without saying a word, he entered his credit card information and hit the order button. "I added Prime. Most of this will be here tomorrow."

"Great."

"There wasn't as much as I thought. Julianna doesn't need more clothes or…" He trailed off.

"I prefer to do that in person. I like to feel what I'm buying her."

"Did you eat?" he asked, his voice level.

"No. I'll heat up some leftovers."

"I brought you soup and a sandwich from the café. I remembered how much you liked their broccoli soup."

"Thank you."

He unpacked the bag, sliding the soup and sandwich in front of me. He opened his, stirring the soup with his spoon.

"Would you rather I ate elsewhere?" he asked.

"No, it's your home, Julian."

He hesitated, then spoke. "I want it to be yours again too."

I sighed, gearing up for another fight. But he pushed my soup closer. "Later, we'll talk. You need to eat and rest."

I'd just picked up my spoon when I heard Julianna cry. Julian was on his feet before I could move. "I'll get her. You eat."

He disappeared, and I dipped my spoon into the steaming bowl, savoring the flavor of the rich and creamy soup. I ate, waiting patiently, wondering what he was doing with the baby. Julian called my name, and I hurried down the hall, stopping in the doorway and trying not to laugh. He had her on the changing table, one hand on her stomach as she squirmed, the other hand holding a misshapen diaper, the tabs torn. He looked at me, slightly panicked.

"I have no idea how to put a fresh diaper on her. She keeps moving and wriggling and flailing her arms. I've ripped two of these things. I don't think she likes me."

I tried not to smile at the expression on his face. I crossed the room, pushing him out of the way. "She hates getting her bum changed. You have to do it fast." I showed him how to slip the diaper under her and fasten the tabs, his intense concentration on the simple task amusing. I tsked at the slight rash on her skin, getting out the cream and putting some on the red marks.

"Is she sick?" he asked.

"No, just reacting. Her urine is a bit strong right now. It'll settle."

I quickly snapped her onesie back into place and wrapped her in a blanket. I turned and held her out. "And she likes you just fine. She's being a baby, Julian. Babies fuss."

He took her, cradling her carefully. "Okay. I thought maybe she was mad at me about acting like an asshole yesterday."

I blinked. "Babies don't 'get mad.' She reacts to the tension I carry, yes. But she doesn't think you're an asshole. She doesn't know what that is. And you shouldn't say asshole in front of her."

He grinned. "You just did—twice."

I had to laugh. He had me there.

"I'm going to finish my soup." I walked past him, taking in a deep breath. "Are you coming?"

He nodded. "Yep."

The rest of the day seemed surreal. The groceries arrived, and he helped put them away. A package came in the late afternoon containing some baby books, and he read one, the book open on his lap, holding Julianna, once again getting the look of intensity on his face.

"Go have a nap," he offered when I yawned. "I have

our girl," he added almost absently, as if it was something he said often.

I headed down the hall, glancing over my shoulder. He was watching me. I felt his stare down to my bones. He had always affected me when he focused his gaze on me, his brilliant-colored eyes darker than usual, the concentration on his face etched into his profile. My breathing picked up not only at his stare but how natural he looked, holding our daughter, cradling her close, his large hand supporting her head. I had noticed him grimace a couple of times when he lifted her, and I wondered if it was from his injury, but I refrained from asking, not wanting to bring up the past yet. He wasn't complaining, so I left it alone. He dropped his gaze, murmuring something to her, and I entered the room and lay on the bed, confused, annoyed, but oddly content. The image of them together drifted through my head as I fell asleep, somehow knowing she was safe with him.

And right now, so was I.

CHAPTER FOURTEEN

Julian

It was an odd day. Filled with moments of levity and humor. Flashes of anger that I tried to tamp down. The hour I spent with Dr. Easton helped. If she was shocked by the news I imparted about Tally and Julianna, she hid it well. She let me vent, offered some suggestions, then told me to go home and try to be a decent human being. And that she would see me in a couple of days.

I was concerned about how exhausted Tally seemed to be, and I blamed myself for a great deal of it. I got her to lie down for a while as I sat on the sofa, reading with Julianna on my lap. Or trying to read. I found her far more fascinating than the book. Every blink, every coo or noise was new and different. She hated having her hands inside the blanket, and I loved how she clutched my finger when I would free one. Our identical eyes would lock, and I wondered if somehow she recognized me. I had never thought of my eyes as beautiful until I saw them in my daughter's face. Now I understood what Tally saw when she looked at me. Or, what she used to see.

I wondered if we could get past this and find each other again. When she got up, she fed Julianna, then brought her back to the living area, sitting with her.

"What is her normal schedule?" I asked.

"Mostly this. Eating, sleeping, pooping," Tally replied dryly. "She's a bit young for gymnastics or dance class."

I laughed. "What else?"

"We walk a lot. I like her to have fresh air on nice days."

"We'll take her tomorrow. It's supposed to be warmer."

She looked confused. "You'll be home?"

"Yes."

"All right."

I held the baby as Tally made dinner. I held her again while we ate. Eating with a baby on your lap was a challenge as I discovered, but I managed, secretly wondering how Tally had done this all by herself. I watched her carefully, my worry growing. Her appetite was still off, although I could see she was trying.

"A few more bites," I encouraged her. I indicated Julianna, who was asleep in my arms. "For her."

I knew better than to snap at Tally or to ask her to eat for my sake. Maybe she would for Julianna's.

She picked up her fork, lifting a piece of chicken to her mouth, chewing listlessly, her gaze focused over my shoulder toward the window. I studied her, wondering what she was thinking. Was she desperate to run? Did she want to talk? I couldn't decide.

When I had gotten the call yesterday, my first emotion was disbelief. By the time I climbed into the helicopter, rage had kicked in. White-hot fury directed at Tally for running from me. Hiding so well I couldn't locate her. Keeping our child—my child—away from me. When I stepped into the room, the rage lessened, and since then, I had vacillated between anger, worry, and confusion. Threats fell from my lips without thought, threats I wasn't sure I could ever follow through on. Awe at the tiny being we had created nudged at my heart. Desire, still hot and strong for this woman, beat under my skin. Profound sadness at what I missed pulsed in the back of my mind. Worry that I was causing Tally stress was eating at me. Leo was right. One of the sites I'd visited while she was busy with Julianna said stress wasn't good for a nursing mother, and it could affect the milk, which affected the baby. I didn't want that to happen.

"Tally," I said quietly.

She looked up, her eyes dull.

"We'll work it out."

"You mean you'll do whatever it takes to keep her and too bad for me."

"I mean we'll work it out. Together." I glanced down at the sleeping bundle in my arms. Warm. Safe. Vulnerable and fragile. Needing her mother because I knew there was no connection in the world like it. "I *won't* hurt you or her." I let those words sink in. "Please. Eat. She needs you."

"I need *her*," she half sobbed, her fear palpable.

I wanted my wife here. My child. But I didn't want it at the expense of a future with Tally. A real future. That would never happen if she was terrified.

I leaned across the table, taking her hand. "You have her. You will always have her. We will figure this out."

"Don't—"

I cut her off. "I won't. We will figure it out." I offered her a smile.

I wasn't sure she believed me, but she picked up her fork and began to eat. I was satisfied with that.

Later, she stood beside me, letting me bathe Julianna. By the time it was over, I was soaked, there was water everywhere, and I learned just how much my daughter loved the water. She kicked her legs, flailed her arms, and splashed everywhere. I held her while Tally washed her hair, not sure enough yet to try that. After, I bundled her, added cream, and changed her diaper fairly successfully. I left Tally to feed her, making sure she had water. I read more of the book, shaking my head at what I didn't know.

I glanced at my watch, surprised to find over two hours had gone by. I went down the hall, peeking into the guest room. A light was on in the corner, and Tally was asleep on her bed, her hair spread around her like wildfire in the sun. Bright and shimmering. More beautiful than I even remembered. Julianna was in her crib, slumbering away, her lips moving and pursing in her sleep. I picked up the blanket from the chair and draped it over Tally, studying her. Even in sleep, I could feel her anxiety. Her hands were clutched tight, her brows drawn down in a frown. Her body looked tense as well. I hunched down, running my hand over her hair, remembering how much that used to relax her. Her hair was as soft as I recalled, and I stroked the curls in long, tender passes, remorse filling me at the pain I could feel inside her.

She had been wrong to run, wrong to hide Julianna from me, but she wasn't without cause. Tomorrow, we would talk and find a starting point. I was determined to win her back.

Her eyes fluttered open, and I smiled. "Hey, baby," I whispered. "Go back to sleep. I was just checking on you."

Julianna began to fuss behind me, and I put a hand on Tally's shoulder as she began to rise. "No, I got her. You sleep." I ran a finger over her cheek. "Let me, Tally. Trust me with her."

She nodded, and without thinking, I bent and kissed her. Just a brief pressing of our lips, but it felt like so much more. It felt like coming home.

I felt her eyes on me as I went to the crib, lifting Julianna. "Hey, baby girl. Hush," I crooned. "Let's go visit and let Mommy sleep, okay?" I rubbed her back the way I'd seen Tally do. "Shh. Daddy has you."

When I glanced back from the door, Tally was still watching. "Sleep," I demanded gently. "I got this. When she's hungry, I'll come get you."

Her eyes shutting was my only response.

It was all I needed.

The next day, I looked around in bemusement. "For something so tiny, you sure need a lot of stuff," I murmured to Julianna. She fretted into her hand, still fussy like the day before.

Tally looked up with a shake of her head. "This is only some of what she needs."

"Why didn't you get all of it?"

She didn't answer, and I knew why. Because she didn't plan on staying.

"Who is June Albright? How did you get her ID?"

She stopped her unpacking and met my eyes. I kept my voice calm and my expression neutral.

"June is the woman I met on the bus when I first arrived. Her boyfriend is a computer geek, and he has all sorts of gadgets and stuff. He duplicated her driver's license so I had a piece of ID to travel here. She purchased my ticket."

"I thought you lost touch with her."

"I never said that." She sighed. "I didn't tell you everything, all right? I kept her and Cathy my secret in case I needed a place to hide again."

"I guess we both kept secrets," I stated mildly.

She didn't respond.

"It's a nice day. Did you want to go for a walk?" I indicated the piece of equipment sitting against the wall that had come off the plane with her luggage. "I assume that attaches to her baby seat thing?"

A smile tugged her lips. "Her carrier. Yes."

"Then let's get some fresh air."

I watched her strap Julianna in, marveling at the ease with which she opened the stroller, locking the carrier in place, adding a blanket, a hat, and pulling up the carrier top so sun wouldn't get into Julianna's eyes. Outside, she let me push the stroller, and we headed to a small park close to the apartment. Julianna cooed and gurgled, her little hands once again finding freedom and flailing. She seemed to be happy outside. More than once, we stopped, and Tally would tuck her hands back inside the blanket, only for Julianna to loosen them again.

"It's a game now," Tally observed.

I bent and chuffed Julianna's chin. "My baby girl is clever." I looked at Tally. "Takes after her mommy."

She looked away, but I saw the gloss of tears in her eyes. Without thinking, I wrapped my arm around her waist and pulled her close. I bent and kissed her forehead, my lips lingering. For a moment, she was stiff, then she relaxed into my side, and we continued the walk that way. One arm around my wife, the other pushing the stroller that held my daughter. Tally held the other side of the handle, and together we kept it straight. It felt right. I felt complete in a way I never had before now.

We sat on a bench, and I walked to the small café and brought back coffee. I handed Tally her cup and sat next to her, peeking in at Julianna. She was asleep, her fist jammed into her mouth the way she liked to do. Her cheeks were pink, her hair sticking out from the hat.

"She looks like you," I observed. "Do you think she'll have your freckles?"

Tally was quick to disagree. "Oh no, Julian. She is you all over again. Even that little dimple that only comes out when you smile really hard. She has your eyes too."

"She is far more delicate-looking than I am," I protested. "Her face is shaped like yours, and she has your mouth and coloring." I nudged her with my elbow. "Let's hope she doesn't get my beard."

Tally laughed as an older woman stopped and peeked into the stroller.

"What a lovely child."

"She looks like her mommy," I said proudly.

Julianna's eyes fluttered open, and she yawned, squirming and impatient. The woman laughed. "Oh, no doubting who her father is with those eyes. She is going to be a heartbreaker when she grows up."

"She isn't dating until she's thirty," I said firmly.

Tally and the woman exchanged a glance and a laugh.

"Good luck with that, Daddy," the woman said before walking away.

Daddy.

It was the first time it had been acknowledged out loud. The word made my throat feel thick.

I focused my gaze on Julianna. "At least thirty," I whispered to her. I met Tally's gaze, and she smiled in understanding. A moment of gentle emotion flowed between us—honest and real. Of course she understood. She smiled every time I referred to her as Mommy.

I finished my coffee and flicked the cup into the waste container beside us. I flinched at the sudden snap of pain. Tally frowned.

"Does it hurt you a lot?" she asked, indicating my shoulder.

"Only at times. There is lingering nerve damage," I admitted.

"I'm sorry."

I acknowledged her words with a dip of my head.

After a few moments of silence, Tally stood. "Let's go, Daddy. She's getting fussy again and will want to be fed soon."

I followed her, still smiling.

Daddy. That was my new favorite word.

Julianna was fussier when we got back to the apartment, and Tally and I took turns walking with her, unable to get her settled.

Tally frowned in worry. "She doesn't want to eat either."

I felt worry in the pit of my stomach. "Is that normal?"

"Not for her." Tally touched her lips to Julianna's forehead. "She's getting warm."

Shortly after, Julianna began to cry. Loud, pitiful wails. She was inconsolable. I had never felt so helpless in my life watching Tally trying to soothe her. We tried a bath, but she didn't even react to the water, which she loved to splash in. Tally went to get her fresh clothes, and I ran my fingers down Julianna's warm cheek as I lifted her to my chest.

"Tell me, baby girl. Tell me what hurts, and Daddy will make it all better."

The only sound was my daughter's cries. My heart broke at the pathetic noises.

Tally came in and frowned. "She's hotter now."

There was no mistaking the worry in her tone.

"We're going to the hospital," I said, handing Julianna to Tally. "I'll go get the car. You bring her downstairs."

She nodded, and I hurried down to the car, already calling Sofia. I told her what was happening, and she assured me I was doing the right thing bringing her in. Then she ordered me to calm down.

"I'm at the ER, and I'll get you in right away. The pediatrician on call is great."

Tally got in the back seat with Julianna, bending close, murmuring reassurances, and rubbing her tummy as her wails became louder. My foot never left the gas pedal, and I gave zero fucks if I got stopped. Luckily, the apartment was close to the hospital, and we were there quickly. Sofia came out and took Tally and Julianna inside, and I found a place in a parking lot, not caring that the guy gouged me. I left the keys and hurried back.

Unsure of my place, I stayed out of the way in the hall, close enough I could go into the room if needed. I paced anxiously, hearing Julianna's crying from behind the door, the muffled sounds like bombs in my heart. My chest ached with her pain.

A woman watched me, catching my eye.

"First one?" she asked.

"Sorry?"

MELANIE MORELAND

"First baby," she replied.

"Yes." I ran a hand through my hair. "She got really hot and was crying. She wouldn't eat." Why I was telling this stranger all that, I had no idea, but I had to talk to someone.

She nodded in sympathy. "They do that. She'll be right as rain soon enough. Probably a little bug or an upset tummy."

I ran a hand through my hair again, then stopped. I could no longer hear Julianna's cries. Panic gripped me until the door opened and I saw Sofia walking toward me, calm and smiling.

"Relax, Daddy," she said. "She'll be fine. She has an ear infection that is causing her discomfort. We gave her something to reduce her fever, and she's already settling."

"Can I see her?"

"Of course."

I followed her into the exam room. Tally was rocking her, murmuring little hushing noises. Julianna was wrapped in a blanket, her eyes shut, nuzzling against Tally. I hunched beside them, covering Julianna's head with one hand and cupping Tally's cheek with the other.

"Our girl has an ear infection?" I asked quietly, feeling relief over such a simple diagnosis.

"Yes. And her tummy is upset. She doesn't feel so well, Daddy."

I glanced up at the doctor who came in. "Can we take her home?"

"Yes. I'll send her some antibiotics, which will help. And keep up with the Children's Tylenol for the fever if needed. She may be a little sleepy or grumpy—" he grinned "—or both. Watch her and come back if you're concerned or her fever goes higher. She should be fine in a couple of days."

Relieved, I took my wife and daughter home.

Twenty-four hours later, I wanted to get my gun and go find someone to shoot. I had never experienced the unending anxiety swirling in my gut the way I had since we'd brought Julianna home from the hospital. She hardly slept unless one of us was holding her, and even then, it was short. She cried and wailed, whimpered and snuffled. She barely ate, only fussing and pushing away. Tally was far calmer than I was, but even she was uptight and anxious. I called Sofia so often, she came to the apartment, checking out Julianna, assuring us she was fine aside from the infection, which was showing signs of improvement.

"The medication needs time to work," she replied to my terse demand as to why Julianna was still so uncomfortable. She looked away, trying not to laugh.

"What?" I snarled.

"I have seen you amid total chaos, Julian. Injured men all around you, yet still in complete control and cool as a cucumber. One little baby with an ear infection, and you're falling apart."

"Those men were not my daughter," I pointed out. "And they never made the noises she does."

She patted my shoulder. "You're a good daddy,

Julian. She'll be fine. Her fever is lower, but her ears hurt and her tummy is upset."

"She poops all the time."

"Again, her tummy is upset. Give it another day, and the improvement will be huge."

"And if it's not?"

"Bring her back to the hospital."

She spoke with Tally, then left, leaving me as frustrated and anxious as before she arrived. I went to the guest room where Tally held Julianna, rocking and humming.

"I'll take her for a bit. You rest."

She hesitated, and I took Julianna from her. "She needs you to be strong. Sofia says by tomorrow we should see a lot of improvement. She'll be hungry. I got in soup from the café. Eat it and lie down."

I walked with Julianna, holding her over my good shoulder. I stroked her back, making low noises in my throat. I didn't want to scare her by trying to sing. That would only make a bad situation worse. Tally looked up from her soup, watching us. I stopped across from her, smiling in reassurance.

"Eat, baby," I encouraged her.

I was shocked when I saw tears forming in her eyes. "No, Tally, please. She'll be fine." I sat beside her, smoothing my hand over her hair. "Everything is going to be fine."

"I don't know how I would have done this without you."

I shook my head. "Probably far better than with me. I'm not very good—"

I was cut off when Julianna spit up, the wet running down my back. Then she filled her diaper to capacity. Overfilled, really. The surplus ran down my shirt, the smell making me gag.

Tally looked startled, and I stared down at the mess on my shirt, flummoxed. I ran a hand through my hair, realizing too late that was a mistake when I felt that the same shit on my shirt was now in my hair.

"I think our daughter is in agreement with me," I said dryly.

Tally started to laugh. Huge peals of amusement burst from her lips. I stood, shaking my head.

"You find me covered in shit amusing, Tally?" I asked, trying not to laugh with her.

"I never imagined I would see the cool, in-control Julian Grayson looking the way you do right now," she admitted between more guffaws.

I caught sight of myself in the mirror on the opposite wall. My shirt was untucked and wrinkled. Covered in baby shit. My hair was everywhere and plastered with the same. I knew the back was wet from spit-up. I stank terribly, and Julianna kept moving, causing more leakage.

I started to chuckle, giving in to the amusement of the situation.

"Finish your soup and lie down. Julianna and I are going for a shower. We both need it."

Her amusement followed me all the way down the hall.

CHAPTER FIFTEEN

Julian

The shower seemed to calm Julianna. I lingered in it, keeping the water warm but not overly hot, the steam seeming to soothe her. Her eyes drifted shut, and she fell asleep. I wrapped her in a large towel and laid her on the bench as I washed off, keeping one hand on her. I was proud of myself as I dried her off, slipped on a fresh diaper and a onesie, all while she slept.

Tally watched from the bed, then held out her arms. I tucked Julianna beside her. "She's asleep, so you sleep," I whispered.

"You need rest too."

"Later." Without thinking, I bent and kissed her forehead. "You're more important. Rest."

Sofia was right, and the next twenty-four hours brought with them a big change. Julianna's fever disappeared, and it was obvious she felt better. Her wide, gummy smile appeared again. She ate. And she showered with me three more times. She loved the water all around her, and I loved bonding with her, making up silly games, and yes, even singing to her. I did it really quietly so Tally couldn't hear me. Julianna liked it, though—I could tell.

While Julianna was napping, I grabbed a longer shower for myself. I towel-dried my hair and walked down the hall, pausing at the door. Tally was standing over the crib, looking down at Julianna, who was sleeping, the silence blissful. I realized, without a doubt, I couldn't bear to hear my daughter cry for any reason. Once she was older and figured that out, I was in trouble.

I watched from the door, something stopping me from going into the room. Then I realized that Tally's shoulders were shaking, and she was covering her mouth to stifle her sobs. I hurried forward, standing behind her.

"What is it? What's wrong?" I asked, terrified.

Tally shook her head and turned, burying herself against my chest. She wrapped her arms around my waist, sobbing hard but quietly. Julianna was fine, her breathing deep and even, the flush gone from her face. "Hey," I whispered, wrapping my arms around Tally, noticing how slight she felt. "What's this? She's fine, baby. By tomorrow, she'll be great."

Tally shook her head, still crying, her voice muffled against my chest. "I know," she hiccuped. "I was just so scared, Julian. And you were so calm and helped us so much…" She trailed off.

I slid my hands up her arms, sliding them over her

neck. I cradled her face in my hands. "I was anything but calm, Tally. Inside, I was terrified. But we worked together, and our girl is going to be fine."

"You-you're a good daddy," she whispered.

I bent and brushed my mouth over hers, tasting her relief in her tears. "You're an awesome mommy. We got this, yeah?"

Her lips trembled, and a shiver rushed down her body. Our gazes locked, her brilliant blue meeting my hazel. Hundreds of words passed silently in the air. Thousands of whispers and hopes. Fears. An entire lifetime of questions and answers flowed between us. A lifetime of us.

Despite my exhaustion, I felt it. The flare of passion I always had when Tally was close. It didn't matter if we were too tired to be making decisions. Too drained to think clearly. I wanted her, and the way her eyes grew larger, her pupils dilating, she wanted me too.

With a groan, I captured her mouth, pulling her tight to my chest. She whimpered, her grip around my waist tightening. I slid my tongue inside, tasting her, the feeling of need growing. She tasted as sweet as I recalled —like candy and Tally. Perfect.

I moved back until I was sitting on the bed, Tally on my lap. She moved her arms to my neck, our mouths fused together. She ran her hands through my hair, tugging hard the way I liked. I gripped her hips, pulling her against my erection. She undulated over me, both of us caught in a vortex of long-lost feelings suddenly come to life and pulsating. She felt right in my arms, different, but right. Like her scent, our daughter had changed her curves, and I wanted to explore them all over again. To know if she was still ticklish. If she liked my tongue on her. Wanted my fingers playing with her. My cock buried inside her. I wanted to discover her all over again.

I fisted her hair, wrapping it around my hand, slanting my head to go deeper into her mouth. Our tongues slid together, a sensual dance. I ghosted my hands up under her shirt, her skin a silken treasure I had missed touching.

Then Julianna woke up, letting out a long wail. Tally and I broke apart, our breathing hard. Her cheeks were flushed, her eyes wide. I cupped her cheek and kissed her again.

"Our daughter is a cockblocker."

Tally giggled, and I stood, laying her on the bed. "Stay."

I picked up Julianna, holding her high on my chest. "Hey, my girl." I carried her to the table and changed her quickly, lifting her back up and carrying her over to Tally. "Ta-da," I murmured, presenting her to Tally with a flourish.

"You're getting good at that."

"Practice."

I settled Julianna beside Tally, surprised when she flailed her arms, squirming against Tally.

"She wants you, Daddy."

Delighted, I scooped her up and rounded the bed, climbing onto the mattress with Tally. I settled Julianna on my shoulder and patted my chest. Tally snuggled into my side, her head under my chin and one hand on Julianna. Both my girls fell asleep, and I grinned as I watched them. Contentment and a feeling of home washed over me, and for the first time in my life, I felt truly at peace. Happy.

I let my eyes drift shut, holding my family.

TALLY

I watched Julian with the baby, his frown of concentration somehow only making him sexier. He had always been handsome, but when he was holding our daughter, he became even more so. She loved being in his arms, as if she knew who he was and that she was safe. I could understand that since I always felt the same way in his embrace. I was so confused. The anger I had felt from him when he walked into the room at the airport had dissolved over the past few days. He was gentle and affectionate with Jules. Patient with me. His passionate kisses yesterday showed me the spark that existed between us was still there. It was, in fact, hotter than ever.

"What's happening between us?" I blurted out, finally addressing the elephant in the room.

He looked up from the bottle he was feeding her, his expression calm. "We're getting to know each other again."

"To what end?"

He set down the bottle, lifting her to his shoulder carefully, rubbing and patting gently on her back the way I had shown him. I was using the pump, getting some milk stored so he, too, could feed her—bond with her in another way.

"To be a family, Tally."

I wasn't sure how to respond, and he spoke again before I could, his tone mild.

"Where have you been?"

I knew I had to be honest with him if I expected him to be the same with me.

"A small place in Nova Scotia. Cathy owns it, and they took me there when I needed a place to stay and be safe."

"Be safe from me?" he asked, his eyebrows lifted.

"Be safe from your world."

Julianna burped loudly, and he praised her, settling her back into his arms and slipping the nipple in again. She began to eat in long pulls. "Why did you come back?"

"Cathy became ill and didn't have much time left. June begged me to come and let her see Julianna. After everything they had done, I couldn't say no. We planned every detail—or, at least, I thought we had."

"You didn't expect to be seen by one of my men."

"Not in the London airport," I admitted.

"So, if Conrad hadn't seen you, you would have left, and I would never know of her existence. You would have hidden her forever."

"Yes."

I met his eyes, seeing the maelstrom of emotions in them despite his calm appearance. "You hate me so much you would have kept her away?"

"I don't hate you, Julian. I wish I did—it would make things so much easier."

"Explain that to me."

"I ran away to protect her. To save her from hurt and pain."

"I'm still not understanding." He glanced down. Julianna had fallen asleep as she often did when feeding. He carefully laid her in the carrier, pulling a blanket around her. He sat back down, facing me, waiting.

"You left me alone," he said simply, but I saw the raw emotion in his eyes. The hurt and pain that clouded his gaze. "Without a word. Not a chance to say goodbye or to explain anything. Injured and alone in the hospital. I didn't know where you were. If you were okay. Why you'd left me. I faced months of recovery on my own. Worried, trying to find you. Terrified something had happened to you. Meeting dead end after dead end." He shook his head. "Even with my connections, it was as if you were a ghost. I had to find a life again."

"I didn't leave until I knew you would recover."

"Which I did alone."

I had trouble meeting his gaze. "I had to go before I changed my mind."

"Well, it's nice to know it at least bothered you a little to walk away."

There was no mistaking the hurt in his voice.

"It tore me apart, Julian."

"Yet, you did it."

I straightened my shoulders. We could go around this for hours.

"And you went back to work. To Hidden Justice."

"I did. In a different capacity, yes."

"What do you mean?"

"I'm only the chess master now, Tally. I move the pieces on the board, but I don't play the game. The bullets that night made sure of that. I can't be in the field at all anymore. I would be a detriment to the team." He drew in a long breath. "And once I fell in love with you, the craving for the edge of danger was gone. I didn't want to risk myself. I didn't want to risk us."

I had noticed the loss of dexterity with his arm. He hid it well, but the occasional grimace crossed his face, and at times when he lifted his arm, I could see a slight tremble in his hand. He often had to switch sides while holding the baby, and I knew his shoulder and arm hurt him. He never said a word, though.

I swallowed, his words echoing in my head. "I hated knowing you were shot because of me."

He cocked his head. "Did you think I would blame you?"

"I didn't know."

"Is that why you ran? You were fearful of me? My reaction?" He shook his head. "When will you realize, Tally, you have nothing to fear from me? In no way do I hold you responsible. Your brother was working his way up the crime ladder and would have been on my radar soon enough. He did this, not you."

I thought back to the night I received the call from Damien. His serious tone telling me I would be escorted to the airport, where a private plane would take me to Julian. How terrified and confused I had been.

"He is badly injured, Tally. He needs you."

Nothing prepared me for seeing Julian lying in a hospital bed, silent and wounded. The tubes, the blood, the unexpected stillness of him. I shut my eyes, shaking my head, trying to clear the vision.

"Damien laid it all on the table. He told me about Hidden Justice. The work you did. How dedicated you were to the cause. How many people you helped to save. Especially women and children. He explained about Elite Security." I swallowed, remembering the horror his next words caused me. "He told me the truth about Dean. What happened that night. And that he had shot Dean dead."

"I'm still pissed at him about that—telling you everything."

"You shouldn't be. He wanted me to know the person you were. How courageous and giving you were. How you risked yourself to make me safe. To make others safe. How dedicated you were to the cause. He wanted me to know the real you in case you died."

Julian frowned, then swallowed.

"The part about Dean—did that upset you? Knowing he was now dead? The kind of person he really was?"

"Knowing how misplaced my trust had been shook me. That he used me, stole my life from me without any remorse, was hurtful. That he tried to kill you horrified me. All of that was a lot to absorb. But what upset me the most was the fact that you had lied all that time. Kept such a huge part of your life a secret. Instead of letting me in so I could maybe help, even if it was emotionally when you did one of these raids, you kept me in the dark." I met his steady gaze. "That's what brought you to the bar that first night—why you drank so much."

"Yes."

"And how you protected me against that biker. Your training."

He nodded, not speaking, simply regarding me the way he did. Intensely, giving nothing away.

"How did you become one of them? Part of Hidden Justice, I mean?" Damien hadn't told me that part.

"I was a rookie in the police. I got shot during a takedown. A street-cop-career-ending injury. Both my knees and my shoulder. I got reassigned to a desk job. I hated it, but I was good at it. I started helping to organize things behind the scenes. It was noticed, and I was contacted by someone at Hidden Justice. Long story short, I met with the man who would become my boss, listened to their objectives, and signed up. I worked my way up fast and got the role of Commander pretty young."

"Can you tell me more about them?"

I shrugged. "They are one of the most hidden agencies there is. Layers and layers of secrets. How they're funded, I have no idea, but their resources are limitless, it seems. I have no clue how they started, who runs the whole show, or how long they've been around. My boss has a boss, who has a boss. How far up that goes, I have no idea. Their mission and goal remain the same and became my objective. Save innocent lives. How they go about it is violent but, frankly, necessary.

That's why governments turn a blind eye. The team became my life."

"And you were dedicated."

"It was easy to be so. Plus, I had no one in my life aside from myself to worry about. Until you."

"And you hid it from me."

"I thought I was protecting you," he admitted. Then he met my gaze. "And you left me because of the omission on my part. You didn't give me a chance to explain—you simply walked away," he stated.

"That was a huge part of it, yes. I was overwhelmed and couldn't think straight. Then I discovered I was pregnant. It-it changed everything."

For the first time, his voice became laced with anger. "How? Did you not think I would rejoice in that news? You never gave me the chance."

I walked over to the carrier, looking down at Julianna, who slept peacefully, unknowing of the chaos around her.

"I was shocked at first and trying to grapple with everything I'd found out. My brother hated me. He couldn't care less if I was dead or alive. You had another whole life I knew nothing about. A scary, dangerous life. You were barely hanging on for a couple of days, and I was already mourning you. When you started to recover, I was so relieved, but I thought about having to go through that again. Of having to explain to our child you were dead if one of your missions went wrong." A tremor ran through me. "My dad died when I was a baby. I didn't know him, so I never missed him. My mom passed when I was a teenager, and I still mourn her to this day. Miss her terribly. I thought if Julianna never knew you, she would never have to know that pain —I could spare her that. I thought that if I walked away now, I would get over you. We would live our lives without you."

"Did that work for you?" he asked.

"No," I admitted.

He stood behind me, his heat wrapping around me. "You didn't think that I would suffer? That I would miss you for the rest of my life?"

"I didn't think I was as important to you as Hidden Justice and your work there."

He settled his hands on my shoulders. "Tally, how could you think that? I loved you."

I heard the past tense and tried not to let my tears escape. "Not as much as I loved you," I whispered.

He spun me in his arms. "You're wrong. I loved you completely. More every day."

"You seemed to be pulling away from me. And you didn't trust me. Not enough to tell me."

"I was wrong. I thought I was protecting you, but the truth was, I was protecting myself. I was afraid, with your history, how you hated violence, you would leave me if you knew how much violence my world contained. The same things that gave me the ability to protect you could also destroy us." He touched his forehead to mine. "And they did."

"I loved you so much, but I was so scared."

"Of me?" he asked again.

"No, of loving you more than you loved me. Of not being enough. Of losing you."

"Tally, how could you doubt my love for you?"

"Because you rarely said it. You loved me with your body, protected me with your actions, but you never said the words. After we got married, it felt as if there was a disconnect between us," I confessed.

He frowned.

"You would leave for 'meetings' and be gone for hours. You didn't let me in, Julian. You seemed so busy with things, but you never let me help. You hid what you were planning from me. I would wait for you for hours, then come home to an empty apartment. When you did come home, you were preoccupied." I ran a hand over my hair. "I thought you were bored with me already. I didn't know what to do. How to reach you. How to be a good wife. I felt as if I was failing. I wondered if you regretted marrying me."

JULIAN

I stared down at her, so many thoughts and feelings swirling in my mind. So many questions, misconceptions, and pain we had to work through.

"Never," I replied. "I never regretted marrying you. The only thing I regret is letting you think I didn't love you as strongly as you loved me. I had planned on telling you everything once I had taken care of the situation. But I was caught up in the discovery of your brother and how despicable he was. Not knowing how to tell you everything you thought about him was a lie. In making plans in case anything did happen to me. A will. The right paperwork at Hidden Justice. I had never had to think about anyone else aside from myself before, and I wanted to make sure you were looked after. Everything seemed to need my attention. I thought you knew—that you understood the depth of my feelings." I slipped my fingers under her chin. "Going forward, I will make certain you know every single day how much I love you."

"Going forward?"

I lifted her hands to my mouth and kissed them. "I need you to forgive me. I need to forgive you. We have to in order to move forward. To build our life together."

She stepped back, shaking her head, walking away. She stopped at the window, crossing her arms. "I can't, Julian. As much as I love you, I can't do this."

"Why?" I asked, fighting down my anxiety and impatience. *What was I missing?*

"It's still there. The danger. What you do."

I frowned.

"I won't take her away. We'll arrange visitation, and you can see her whenever you want. But I can't live with the fact that one day I'll get a call from Damien, and this time, you won't come back to us. I need to build my own life."

I approached her, shaking my head. "Listen to me. I am *not* doing ops anymore. I meant it when I said your brother ended that for me. I work from my desk. I don't even join the team for outside recon. Nothing. I can't pull a gun fast enough or rely on my arm to be steady enough to pull the trigger. I am nothing but a shadow. I assign the men. Debrief and help them. That is all."

"And when that isn't enough? When you decide to go back out there?"

"I won't. I have too much to live for."

"But you won't give it up."

I inhaled deeply. "If you ask me to, I will. For you."

"Then you would resent me."

"I don't know what the future holds, but I do know I want you in it. If that's what you need, I'll do it."

She glanced away. "Love shouldn't have conditions."

"Sometimes life is just that way."

Julianna woke up and began to fuss. Tally moved around me, picking her up. She rocked her, making hushing noises to soothe our daughter, but her own eyes were troubled.

"Tally," I began, waiting until she looked up and met my gaze.

"You say you wanted to spare Julianna the pain of losing me, the pain you've been struggling with since you lost your mother."

She nodded.

"Would you trade that pain for the loss of the memories you have of her?"

For a moment, she looked confused, then her eyes flared with understanding. "No," she choked out.

"She could lose you the same way you lost your mother. I could be crossing the road tomorrow and be hit by a car." I studied her as my words sank in. "Life isn't guaranteed or wrapped up in a bow, baby. You can't shield her from it, no matter how much you want to."

I could see my words hit their mark.

"I need to think," she murmured.

"Promise me you won't leave."

"I won't. But I need time."

She walked down the hall, her shoulders bent. I shook my head, wondering if it was too late. If my lies and her running had already broken us. Matteo had warned me breaking her trust would have consequences. Could she forgive me? I had already forgiven her. Listening to the pain in her voice when she talked about her reasons. Although I didn't totally understand them, I knew to her they were very real and very strong. She had been scared. She still was. What I had said to her had rattled her.

I sat down, feeling despair.

Only time would tell.

Later that night, I heard Julianna fussing, and I slipped into the room, laying my hand on her tummy and running it in circles. She settled immediately, the light touch soothing her. Tally had shown me that trick. I glanced toward the bed, surprised to find it empty.

I headed to the living room, finding Tally staring out the window into the inky darkness of the night. Her thin cotton gown ended at her knees, and her shoulders were bare. I stepped behind her, drawing her back into my arms. Her skin was chilled.

"What are you doing?" I asked quietly, unable to resist pressing a kiss to her shoulder.

"I hurt you," she whispered. "I was so scared and confused, I hurt you and Julianna with my selfishness." She drew in a shaky breath. "I thought if I left you first, the pain wouldn't be as bad since I controlled it. That I wouldn't miss you every day. Long for you every day. Want to share every little discovery of her with you."

Despite the pain in her voice, my heart soared at her admission. I tightened my arms around her but didn't speak.

"My whole pregnancy, I missed you. I took pictures all the time, wrote a journal like I was talking to you, sharing the time with you."

"I would like to read it."

"You're right, Julian. I wouldn't give up my memories of my mom to erase the pain. I wish I had memories of my dad." Her voice caught in a sob. "I-I never thought of it that way."

"I know, baby. I understand."

She spun in my arms, peering up at me. Her eyes were red-rimmed and filled with tears. It was obvious she had been crying for a long time. "How can you be so forgiving? You must hate me," she sobbed.

I cradled her face in my hands as I shook my head. "I can't hate you, baby. I know you were scared and confused. I know your first instinct was to run. I hate the fact that I missed your pregnancy and Julianna's birth. I hate knowing how alone and scared you've been. How much you've been handling on your own." I pressed my forehead to hers. "But I can't hate you," I repeated. "I love you too much."

She gripped my wrists. "Still?"

I met her gaze, letting her see the emotion in my eyes. Wanting her to feel the depth of the feelings I had for her. "Always," I vowed.

Then my mouth was on hers, our lips moving together. I tasted the salt of her sadness, the sweetness that was her. I pulled her tight to my chest, devouring her mouth, my need and desire for her overwhelming everything else.

She wrapped her arms around me, and I felt every inch of her through the thin material of her gown. I lifted her into my arms, our mouths never separating. I carried her to my room, laying her on the bed, following her down to the mattress, my weight pinning her down. We kissed endlessly, reacquainting ourselves with each other. The nuances of her mouth, the soft shape of her lips underneath mine. All were as new and different as they were familiar and comforting.

I trailed my mouth across her cheek to her ear. "I want you."

"Yes," she replied, tugging at my shirt. "Yes, Julian."

Seconds later, we were skin-to-skin, my heat soaking into her chilled flesh. I rediscovered everything I had forgotten, every memory of her I had tucked away in the dark recesses of my mind. The tiny group of freckles on her right breast I loved to tease with my tongue. The dimples on her elbows and knees. How dainty and elegant her ankles were under my fingers. The rounded curves where her hips met her waist and how ticklish she was. The sweet indent between her thighs where she was wet and ready for me. How she whimpered when my tongue touched her heat. She gasped my name, the longing in her voice ramping my passion higher.

She gripped at my shoulders and sank her fingers into my hair, yanking on the strands. She arched her back, pushing herself closer to my tongue. I lapped and teased, sliding one finger inside her, then two, riding out her unexpected orgasm. My cock was hot and heavy, aching to be joined with her. She shocked me when she pushed on my chest, and I fell back on the bed with a wry grin. My wife wanted to reacquaint herself with me as well.

I groaned as her eager mouth sucked on my nipples. I shivered as her blunt nails traced patterns on my skin. She nipped at my neck with her teeth, then followed the sting with a soothing swirl of her tongue. She pressed kisses to my new scars, her mouth lingering over them, tender and sweet. I cupped her face and kissed the tears that tracked down her cheeks, knowing the reason for them. The touches of her mouth were like small, healing balms on the marred flesh.

She teased and licked her way down my body, wrapping her hand around my erection.

"Oh God, Tally, yes, yes," I groaned when her hot mouth slid over the head of my dick, her talented tongue swirling as she took me deep into the wetness of her throat. I arched my back, wanting more of her. I looked down, meeting her gaze. Wild blue met my dazed hazel, the expression and depth of passion in her eyes shaking me to the core.

"I need to be inside you. Now," I demanded. "*Now*, Tally."

She straddled me, guiding me to her center. She sank down, inch by glorious inch, until we were fused together. She rolled her hips, bracing herself on my chest, the movement making me hiss in pleasure. I gripped her thighs, encouraging her. "Ride me, Tally. Take what you want, baby. I'm yours."

Her eyes darkened and she moved. Long, deep rolls of her hips. I thrust upward, matching her rhythm, not wanting to be separated from her. Her head fell back, small whimpers of pleasure escaping from her mouth. With a low roar, I sat up, gathering her close. We rocked and moved. Loved and fucked. She moaned my name as I tipped us over, lifting her legs to my shoulders, and began to thrust into her powerfully. She tightened around me, her muscles fluttering and seizing as she came hard, crying my name. I buried my face in her neck as ecstasy overwhelmed me. My orgasm was powerful, crashing into me like a tidal wave, sweeping my feet out from under me and leaving me twisting in the powerful current, unable to tell up from down as my world spun out of control.

Until it crested and I was at peace. Wrapped in my wife's arms, my weight once again pressing her into the mattress. She held me tight, stroking my damp back with her gentle hands, murmuring my name.

I lifted my head, meeting her gaze.

"Stay," I whispered. "We'll work it out, Tally." I kissed her. "Don't leave me alone again."

"I won't, Julian."

"I love you."

She smiled. "I love you too."

CHAPTER SIXTEEN

Julian

T ally glanced across the table, her gaze anxious. I met her eyes, offering her a smile.

"What, baby?"

After we'd made love last night, I'd carried her back to the guest room and slid into the bed with her.

"I want you back in our bed."

"I won't be able to hear her," Tally protested. *"And I've read about how people can hack the monitors. It's scary."*

"I'll get Damien to make one. His will be unhackable."

"Okay."

"So, you'll move back to our room? Turn this into a nursery?"

"Yes."

I kissed her again, wanting to make love with her once more, except Julianna wanted to be fed. After that, Tally fell asleep, exhausted. My cockblocking child got me again.

"Are you going to work today?" she asked.

"For a while this afternoon."

She looked away.

"Hey," I called softly. "Elite needs to be looked after.

I have to make sure everything is okay with Hidden Justice. It's administrative stuff, Tally. Honest."

Then I had an idea. "You should come with me. I'll show you."

"Really?"

"Yes. Maybe if you see what I do, you can relax."

"All right."

"Let me clear up the backlog today, and you can come tomorrow. I'll take my girls to lunch after."

She continued to look hesitant, and I knew how worried she still was. "It'll be fine, Tally. You'll understand more tomorrow."

She picked up her coffee cup and took a sip.

"Today, you can go online and order more stuff for Jujube. And whatever you need."

She sputtered. "Jujube?"

I grinned. "I called Julianna that last night, and she giggled. I swear she did—either that, or it was my singing. But I'm going with the name, and I'm using it." I lifted one eyebrow, teasing. "Seems to me you liked that name."

She chuckled. "Yes, I did."

Then she sobered. "I have to go back to Nova Scotia, Julian."

"What?" I asked, shocked. "I thought we agreed—"

She cut me off. "I have to close the house, get our things."

"No. I'm not letting you out of my sight again."

"I'm not asking permission."

I narrowed my eyes, studying her. She returned my stare, hers open and honest. "I'm not staying there. But

I can't just leave the place unoccupied and abandoned. I owe June and Cathy better than that."

I relaxed at her words. She wasn't leaving me. She was closing up that chapter of our past. "I'll come with you."

"Okay," she agreed readily.

"How long would you need?"

"A couple of days. There isn't a lot of stuff. We lived pretty simply."

"How *did* you live?" I asked curiously. "You didn't take any money with you."

"I had money I had saved. Cathy refused rent. I paid the utilities in cash. I worked while I could at a little place that paid me cash. I wasn't sure what I was going to do once Jules got older, but I was still taking it one step at a time." She shrugged, looking chagrined. "My thought process was way off. I wasn't really planning, just surviving."

"Baby brain. Pregnancy fog." I nodded as I spoke. "I read about it."

A smile curled her mouth. "I see."

"No more surviving," I said firmly. "You're my family. I'll take care of you. Both of you."

"I'm not on birth control," she burst out.

My eyes widened in shock. I hadn't even thought about that last night. "Tally," I breathed out.

"I'm sure it's all fine. I hear it's harder to get pregnant when you're breastfeeding…" She trailed off.

"You were on birth control when you got pregnant."

"I missed a pill."

"One missed pill and you got pregnant. You're on

nothing now, and we made love twice last night. Odds are pretty good—" I stopped talking and looked meaningfully at her stomach.

She looked stricken.

"Would it be awful, Tally? Another Jujube?"

"Unexpected."

"You'll have me this time. I'll be right beside you every step."

"Let's not jump to conclusions. We'll see what happens," she murmured.

I leaned over her and kissed her. "I'll get some condoms."

"You do that."

I managed to contain my grin until I was walking away. The thought of her being pregnant again didn't upset me. Not a single bit.

Tally was surprisingly nervous the next day when we got to the office. I introduced her to Anne and showed off Jujube. If Anne was shocked about the sudden appearance of a wife and child, she kept it to herself. I did soften the shock by telling her we had been separated and I never spoke of it as it was personal. She accepted that and was warm and friendly to Tally. When we stepped into my office and shut the door, I tried to hold in my laughter as Tally glanced at my desk, horrified at the chaos.

"You need to fix that?" I asked.

"No," she replied, her gaze never leaving the surface

covered in files, coffee cups, scattered paper clips, and other items strewn around it. She was still a neat freak, our apartment more organized than it had been since the day she'd left. She was constantly puttering.

Her eyes grew round when I pressed the lever for the secret panel and it slid open.

"Hidden Justice," I said simply.

She stepped in, and I followed with Julianna dozing in her carrier. Tally walked around the space, studying the walls, the maps and grids lined up on the panels. I sat at my desk and switched on the monitors, checking the building, my fingers flying over the keyboard as I flipped through the various areas. As usual, it was peaceful and secure.

Tally came over, glancing at the screens. "You watch everything from here?"

"I make sure everything is in its place. Damien sweeps it constantly. So does Leo."

"So not just IT and building manager, then."

"No. Two of the best agents I've worked with. I trust them implicitly. As I do all the men I use for Elite." I went on to explain the concept behind Elite. Tally smiled.

"You look after them."

"I give them a different way to live where they're useful and needed." I met her gaze. "Hidden Justice is not a lifelong thing, Tally. For any of us. The emotional toll is too exacting."

She nodded, her eyes widening as she looked at the middle screen. "That's the outer office where I worked."

"Yes. I check on Anna on occasion."

She narrowed her eyes. "How often did you check on me?"

I pulled her down to my lap, kissing her. "All the time. You fascinated me. I loved watching you. I learned so much just observing you."

"Stalker," she muttered.

"Yep. I was addicted." I pulled her close, nuzzling my face into her neck. "Still am."

She shivered.

"Do you know how often I fantasized about having you in here? Bending you over my desk and taking you?" I murmured, kissing her throat. "This office, the other office. Some days, I had to leave before I dragged you in and did just that."

"I would have let you."

With a groan, I crashed my mouth to hers, instantly losing myself in the vortex of sensation and passion. I fisted her curls, kissing her harder, deeper—wanting more.

Damien walked in, stopping when he saw us.

"Oh, I'll, ah, come back."

Tally scrambled off my lap, and I waved him in. "It's fine."

He looked uncomfortable, and I realized it was the first time he had seen her since she'd left me. He'd been the one to tell her everything. She solved the issue by giving him a hug. He squeezed her back, murmuring something. She drew back, shaking her head.

"We're good," she said. "We're good, Damien."

He bent and chuffed Julianna under the chin. "Wow, I know who your daddy is," he teased.

I laughed. "You got that right."

Damien sat down, placing a box on my desk. "Everything you wanted."

"Everything?"

"Yep."

I lifted the lid and handed Tally a new cell phone. "It's secure and has all my numbers programmed in."

"Mine too, in case," Damien added.

"Okay," she agreed, looking at the top-of-the-line phone.

"I'll show you all the features tonight," I promised.

I pulled out a monitor, and he explained to us how to use it and how he'd made it secure. He slid an envelope my way, which I slipped into my pocket. Tally noticed it, but she didn't ask until later that night.

"What was in the envelope?"

I didn't lie. "Untraceable tracking devices."

"You're going to track me?"

"Yes. As a precaution."

"You don't trust me not to run?"

I leaned forward and kissed her. "Yes, I trust you completely or I would have hidden the fact that I have them. It's a precaution. We all have them. I'll put one on her stroller and in your purse, maybe a few other places. If you ever lose something, we can find it." I kissed her again. "If you're ever lost, I can find you."

"Oh." She sighed and lifted a shoulder. "Fine, then."

"I doubt we'll ever need them, but…" I let my voice trail off.

She nodded. "I get it. You're covering all the bases."

I squeezed her hand. "Yes."

She stood. "I'm going to bed." She glanced over her shoulder. "Or I guess I don't have to tell you that. You probably have one of those on my butt. You patted it a lot earlier. I thought you were copping a feel, but now I know. Shame. I might have let you pat it some more. Get to yet another base."

With a wink, she sauntered down the hall. I laughed at her words and stood, following her. I had been copping a feel, and I was determined to do it again, except this time, I wouldn't stop until she was groaning my name.

And I didn't need a tracking device to figure out how.

CHAPTER SEVENTEEN

Julian

Two weeks later, I pulled on my jacket, straightening my sleeves. Tally tugged on my collar, smoothing my tie. "I love how hot you look in a suit."

I yanked her close and kissed her. She was rumpled and sleepy-looking from our lovemaking earlier. Her hair was mussed, her eyelids heavy, and her mouth swollen and pink.

"I prefer being naked with you," I said against her mouth.

She slapped my chest. "Go to work."

"You still plan on coming by for lunch?"

"Yes. I want to ask Damien a few things about this phone."

I held back my chuckle. She was finding the new phone a challenge with all the things it could do.

Things were going so well. Tally was relaxing, finally accepting what I had been telling her. That my role had changed with Hidden Justice and I was in the background. Safe. She was settling into our new life, and we were finding our way. I was open and honest with her, even having her come into the office a couple of times to help me organize things so she saw firsthand what I did.

I showed her every day how much she meant to me. Talked to her, made love to her. Said the words she needed to hear. Every day, I saw a little more of her walls come down. More sparkle in her beautiful eyes. More trust between us.

We were slowly finding our way back to each other.

And our daughter was our focal point. Our common ground. I was crazy about her. She fascinated me as much as her mother did. They had become my world, and I loved spending time with them.

"Are you going to pick up a test today?" I asked.

She shook her head in amusement since I'd been asking her the same thing daily. I used condoms now, but I wanted to know if she was pregnant. She told me we had to wait as it was too early until now.

"Yes, I'll pick one up."

I grabbed her hand, holding it to my chest. "Wait until I get home to take it, okay? Or you can take it in my office. I want to be there, either way."

"Fine," she mumbled.

I lifted her chin, meeting her eyes. "Together, right?"

That was our new motto.

She nodded. "Together."

Later that day, Damien sat across from me in the back office. He was glowering as he looked at his laptop, and he answered his phone with a frown on his face. He listened for a moment, his glower getting deeper.

"When?" he snapped.

I was shocked at the furious expression on his face and the cold tone in his voice. Something was wrong. Very wrong.

"And I'm just hearing about it now? How the fuck did that happen? What did they get?" He listened for a moment.

"Well, find out and call me back. I need to know everything. Every motherfucking keystroke."

He slammed his cell phone down.

"What's going on?"

"There was a breach in security at the office in Montreal."

"A breach?" I responded.

"Someone hacked in to the system. They were shut down fast, but they're scrambling trying to figure out what info they got."

"What sector were they in?"

"Past cases."

Something clutched at my stomach, but I ignored it. "They can't get names, right? Everything is encrypted."

His fingers flew over the keyboard. "That's what I'm trying to figure out."

"Only that office?"

"Nothing in ours," he assured me. "I have ours locked down tighter than Fort Knox. I warned them to tighten a couple of their protocols."

"Good."

He froze. "They got past the encryptions. All of them. They got into one case. One name. They hacked in to the files of one name."

He met my eyes. "Yours."

Then my phone rang. I hit speaker, the sound of my daughter crying and Tally's shallow breaths filling the air. I met Damien's gaze again, already on my feet, dread filling my chest.

"Tally," I said calmly. "Why is the baby crying?"

A sob was my response. Everything in me froze. My body locked down, ice shooting through my veins. Damien immediately began to type, and I knew he was tracking her. I forced myself to talk.

"Tally, what's wrong? Where are you? Are you lost?" I asked as if everything was normal. I knew I needed to keep her on the line as long as possible.

"J-Julian, help us," she breathed out. "They-they took us…*please*."

I leaned close to the speaker. "Stay calm, baby. Who took you?"

A male voice filled the air. "So, Mr. Grayson, it appears I have something of yours you might want back."

"Who is this?"

"Someone from your past."

"I have a lot of past. You'll have to be more specific."

"It doesn't matter."

"I think it does," I retorted. "You take my wife and child, every detail matters."

He laughed, the sound menacing. "Does the name Zander ring a bell?"

I met Damien's startled gaze across the desk.

"Zander is dead. I saw it with my own eyes."

"Call me a fan. Someone wanting to avenge him."

"And how does taking my wife and child help you in that cause?"

"I have something you want, and you can get me what I want."

"Which is?"

"Marcus Gallo."

I tightened my hands into fists, wrapping them around the edge of the desk to stop myself from losing it. The only way he could have seen that information was if he was responsible for the hacking.

"What makes you think I know where he is?"

His laughter once again sent shivers down my spine. His voice was pitched low when he responded. "Oh, *Commander*, I think you know where everyone is."

For a moment, I couldn't speak. Whoever this was had obtained more than names from the security breach.

"Let me speak to my wife."

"Julian?" she whispered, her voice thick with tears. "I'm scared."

"I know," I soothed, trying to keep the fear out of my tone. "It's going to be okay, Tally. I promise."

"Julian, I need you to stop playing chess."

I shut my eyes, knowing what she was saying. She didn't want me to simply move the pieces around the board this time. She needed me to come and get her. *Me.*

"The game is over, baby. I'll get you. Both of you."

I heard a small gasp as the phone was taken away, and he was back on the line. "You have thirty-six hours to contact Marcus and get him here. I'll call with further instructions."

"You harm one hair on my wife's or child's head, you're a dead man."

"I wouldn't be making threats if I were you."

"It's not a threat, it's a promise. And I want a call in six hours so I can hear my wife's voice."

He hung up.

I looked at the phone, then at Damien.

"Thirty-six hours," he repeated.

"He'll be dead in twenty-four, and my family will be safe. You have the trackers up?"

"Yes."

"Are they active?"

"Yes."

"Get me a location, and I want eyes and ears. Now."

I picked up the private, secure phone and dialed a number, not caring what time of the day it was in that part of the world.

"Julian," Matteo's voice greeted me. "Marcus and I were just—"

I interrupted him. "Someone's taken Tally and the baby. They want Marcus in exchange."

For a moment, I heard silence on the line. Then Marcus spoke.

"We'll be there as fast as we can."

I hung up.

My office resembled a war zone. Schematics and maps hung on the walls. Profiles of the men we knew were responsible for this. The best of the best of my agents filled my office. The most elite men I had chosen personally to get my family back safely were in full mission mode. All the doors were open, the sounds of their voices and footsteps filling the hallways. Anne was safe at home, none the wiser after Leo told her there was a gas leak and not to come back until he called her. Egan and Damien sat together, mapping out the explosives that would finish the job once we were all safe. Egan hadn't hesitated when Marcus called him, showing up ready to party.

Thanks to the small, undetectable trackers I had placed on Tally's possessions, the baby carrier, and diaper bag, we knew exactly where they were. The perps had disabled the more obvious one on her phone, not thinking there would be more. It only proved how inept and careless they were. Bent on revenge, going off half-cocked, high on hacking in to a system they shouldn't have been able to get into, they were reckless but still dangerous. They would be until my family was back with me, safe.

In a matter of hours, we had eyes and ears on the building where they were being held captive. A broken-down semi caused a distraction while a man slipped around back and planted eyes for us in the corners of dirty, cracked windows. From an abandoned building across the street, heat imaging showed us where my family was in the building and how many targets there were. Silent drones landed on the roof, the sounds in the building coming through laptops. Everything was recorded, traced, and noted. We were taking no chances.

We knew there were fourteen of them and nine of us. Good odds.

For us.

Damien had tracked down the group of Zander followers. Just a bunch of chatter and low-level background noise until now. Crackheads who thought Zander was a god among men and wanted to emulate him. Create their own perfect families and rule together. We had a profile on each of them, and tonight, their visions would end. Along with their lives. The remaining dregs of Zander who would forever be extinguished.

That was the hope I clung to.

There had been no more phone calls. But a picture appeared on my phone of Tally and Julianna. Tally was holding her, huddled in a corner, her expression filled with fury.

"Keep being mad, baby," I muttered. *"Stay calm. I'm coming."*

Anger, frustration, and barely concealed rage kept me going. I cursed myself and my pride. My arrogance. I had insisted I was invincible. Hidden. That I was safe. My family was safe. Because of my refusal to see the danger, I had opened up the two people I loved more than life itself to that danger. Tally had been right.

The sound of heavy footsteps made me look up. Matteo and Marcus walked in. Both tall and broad, wearing matching ferocious expressions, their shoulders back, ready to fight. They had to be exhausted, but all I saw on their faces, and in their postures, was determination.

I moved forward, extending my hand to each of them. I received a hard handshake as well as a bear hug from Marcus before I spoke.

"We're ready. You won't be in danger," I assured him.

He snorted, trying to lighten the atmosphere. "As if I was worried. We're here to let loose a little. Shoot some bad guys like the old days."

Matteo grinned, shaking his head. "The island is far too quiet. I need some target practice." Then he rested his hand on my shoulder, his dark gaze intense. "Your family will be back with you soon. I promise you that."

I swallowed before I replied. "Yes, they will." I met Marcus's gaze. "And you'll be back with yours."

He nodded. "And I think maybe that visit is going to be moved up."

"Absolutely." There was no question now. I had to make sure of their safety.

"Whoever this is has to be some talented hacker. You need to drill down deep into the system for names. The firewalls and security are almost invincible."

"Almost." I grimaced. "He found a way in. Damien is furious."

Marcus grinned. "No doubt he will set them straight."

Damien glanced up. "Damn right. I'm in on this one. It's personal." Then he muttered something about systems and breaches, his anger evident.

Marcus put his hand on my shoulder. "Tell us the plan."

CHAPTER EIGHTEEN

Julian

The wind blew around us, sending dry leaves and dirt tumbling around the dead grass and concrete that surrounded the old, abandoned building. Clouds obscured the moon, the night dark and foggy.

Perfect for a raid.

We blended with the dark, all dressed in black, nothing to be seen except our eyes. We were silent and stealthy. Shadows in the dark. Armed to the teeth, ready to kill anyone standing in our way of taking back what was mine.

Tally was in the back room, closest to the loading dock. They, no doubt, thought it was the easiest way to get her into the building with no one seeing her. It was also the easiest way for me to take her out of it.

Dim light glowed behind the dirty windows, not easily seen from the street, the building looking empty.

We knew it was not.

The screech of a night owl echoed in the quiet, and I waited patiently until another sounded. The guards around the building were gone. Eight taps echoed in my ear, and I knew we had eight heat sources remaining, plus Tally's and Julianna's in the back. I closed my eyes and prayed we'd be successful. That my shoulder and arm would cooperate and stay strong long enough for me to see this mission through. Sofia had jabbed my shoulder with a syringe filled with a mixture of pain relievers, numbing action, and whatever else she could add to give me freer motion and hopefully a steady hand when I aimed my gun if I needed it.

I gave a low whistle, indicating it was time.

We waited to hear the commotion around the front of the building that took out the guards, then we slipped inside the door in the basement, working our way up to the main floor by the loading dock. The building was cold, rank, and disgusting. It ratcheted up my anger to unchecked fury, knowing my wife and baby daughter had been trapped in here for hours, no doubt terrified and freezing.

"On the left," a voice whispered in my ear. "All the remaining heat signals are in one place."

I walked in, my gun already aimed, my arm steady. Matteo was with me, his gun drawn, flanking my side. I growled low in my chest at the sight before me. Tally holding Julianna, terror bleeding from her eyes. Behind her, a Zander look-alike, his gaunt frame and bleached-blond hair giving him a ghoulish skeleton look. He held a gun to my wife's head, and images from the day Marcus and Missy took down Zander floated through my mind from the videos I had seen. It was like déjà vu, except I didn't have Missy and her wicked knife skills to back me up. But I had something else.

His voice was cracked and high, his eyes wild as he observed us. "I wasn't expecting you so soon. How rude to show up early." He shook his head, looking mournful. "You could have made this easy, but now I have to kill all of you and find that coward myself." He tsked.

Marcus strolled in the doorway on the other side of the room. "No, you don't, asshole. Freddy, isn't it?"

Freddy's eyes went wide, shock and hate registering. "It's Fredrick," he snapped.

Marcus waved off his words. "You want me, *Freddy*? You come get me. Step out from hiding behind a woman and her child like the coward you are and face me."

I caught Tally's gaze, slowly lowering my hand. I saw understanding on her face and her barely discernible nod.

I took in the room. The other look-alikes—all too young, too stupid to be caught up in a game like this—held their guns wrong, their anxiety obvious as they surrounded Marcus. They would be easy to take out. We needed to distract Freddy so Tally would be safe.

As if he knew that, he gripped her tighter, using her as his shield.

Marcus stepped closer, making Freddy focus on him.

"How did you find me?" Marcus asked, almost casually.

"I wanted to avenge Zander. He understood what it was like to be trapped, ignored. He didn't deserve to die like a dog in the street."

"You're right. He deserved worse."

Freddy grew agitated, shifting. His grip loosening slightly on Tally. I noted it, hoping for a little more slack so she could drop to the floor.

"I taught myself to be a hacker growing up. I spent months searching every trail I could find that mentioned him. I wanted to know who killed him. There was an odd notation in one file. It took me a long time to figure out. I searched and searched and found just enough crumbs to lead me to Hidden Justice. That took me endless hours of effort before I was able to find a crack. But it was all I needed. I slipped in twice before they figured it out, burrowing down layers and encryptions. By the time they were onto me and locked me down, I had what I needed." He focused on Marcus. "And now I'm going to end you." He laughed. "All of you. The elite of the righteous Hidden Justice. Zander would be so proud."

"Let me tell you about Zander," Marcus said, crossing his arms. "He was a psychotic bastard with ideas of grandeur who liked to beat women and sell them. Nothing about him deserved respect or remembrance."

"Shut your mouth!" Freddy yelled, furious, his attention entirely on Marcus. I saw movement out of the corner of my eye and knew Damien was ready. I inched forward, preparing myself.

"He was right—we need to choose our families. Breed them and train them. Make them in our own images. We will create perfection—"

Marcus cut Freddy off. "He was a coward and a

murderer. Sick in the head. Twisted, insidious, and the world was safer once he was dead. The world has no idea he even existed. It'll be the same for you."

Freddy began shaking in his fury. He became distracted, which was what we wanted. He waved his gun, practically panting in his anger. Marcus continued to goad him as I inched closer, Matteo remaining where he was.

"My wife silenced his voice with a knife through his throat. I ended him with a bullet to his head. In the end, he died the same way he lived. Violently and without purpose. He wasn't so high and mighty when he was drowning in his own tainted blood. He lived in the dark, and he died in the dark. I hope he's burning in hell." Marcus's eyes glittered. "You can say hi when you join him."

It happened in two seconds. Freddy lost his cool, pushing Tally away, aiming his gun toward Marcus. I lunged, catching my wife before she fell to the floor, dragging her and Julianna away, shielding them with my body. There was a hail of gunshots behind us, the noise deafening. Julianna began to wail, and Tally shook uncontrollably under me. I pressed my lips to her ear. "It's over, baby. I promise, it's over."

I lifted my head. The men who did this were all on the floor, dead. Freddy was on his back in front of Marcus, blood covering his chest, a hole in the middle of his forehead from Damien's gun. As soon as he'd had a clear shot, he had taken it from his vantage point behind us—just as we planned. Marcus watched as I rose to my feet, helping Tally up, making sure she didn't see the carnage behind us. Matteo took her other arm, and we headed to the door.

"Don't look, Tally," I urged. I didn't want her to see it—to have the memory of the blood and dead bodies in her head.

She shook so hard, I bent and scooped her and Julianna up in my arms, hurrying out to the van that was waiting. She shut her eyes, turning her face to my chest. In the van, I wrapped her in warm blankets, rocking her and Julianna. Unbidden tears filled my eyes, relief overwhelming me. I had them. They were safe.

I only prayed Tally could move past this. That I hadn't lost her once and for all.

———

"Is that how it happens all the time?" Tally asked. She was curled up in the corner of the sofa, a blanket wrapped around her. Sofia had checked her and Julianna out, assuring me they were fine, although Tally's body temperature was low. She had used all the blankets and her own sweater to make sure Julianna was warm enough. Now I was looking after *her*. The blankets, hot soup, coffee, and a heating pad around her feet were slowly getting her back to normal. She was shockingly pale, and she trembled a lot. I was certain some of it was residual fear. Julianna was cranky but had finally settled and was asleep in my arms. I couldn't put her down or move away from Tally. It was impossible. I wasn't sure when I would be able to do so for a long time.

I shook my head. "Usually, they're faster. But we didn't know what we were walking into. We suspected that coward would use you as a shield, and your safety was paramount."

"Were you really going to give him Marcus?"

"No. We wanted his presence to distract him so Matteo could set up for the kill shot. Matteo was second to shoot him if Damien couldn't get the right angle. I was last." I patted my shoulder. "I wanted to kill him myself for daring to touch you. To frighten and threaten you and our daughter. But I worried I wouldn't have the control, and it was too important. Better him dead and you safe than me being the one to pull the trigger."

She shivered. "He was awful. His eyes were empty."

"So was his soul."

"He's really dead?" she whispered, playing with the edge of the blanket.

I reached for her hand. "Yes. All of them are. Damien has his laptop and is tracing every step to make sure there are no others. Everyone involved is dead and the building demolished."

Tears filled her eyes.

"What?"

"Their families. They'll always wonder…"

I stroked her cheek, in awe of her compassion. She knew that feeling, and she didn't want others to suffer the same way.

"None of them had family, Tally. All were loners with no close ties. That's what they were searching for. We always check, and if they've left someone behind, we make sure they know."

"You think of everything."

"We try to minimize the pain for people who are innocent bystanders. They don't need to suffer because of someone else. In many ways, family and friends are victims too. They have no idea what the person was capable of. We just allow them to be able to grieve and move on."

"So, it's really over."

"Yes. You're safe, baby. Both of you."

I drew in a deep breath. "You'll be safer tomorrow."

She frowned. "Tomorrow?"

"I'm sending you and Julianna with Marcus and Matteo to the island. It's protected and safe. They'll look after you."

"What about you?"

I met her eyes. "You can recover and decide if you want me to join you. After today—" I shifted closer "—I realize how arrogant I was, thinking I was untouchable. That the danger I was used to in my world of Hidden Justice would never touch you. I should have known better. I watched it affect the lives of my agents. How close both Matteo and Marcus came to losing the women they loved because of it. I convinced myself I was different. I was behind the scenes, so of no interest…"

"Until a madman changed your mind." She finished for me.

"I will never forgive myself." I sighed. "And I know you were already wary and scared. I'm sure you need time to think and reflect. Decide."

"I think I understand what you do more now. How vital it is and why you were so dedicated."

I furrowed my brow in confusion.

"While I was sitting there, waiting for you—because I knew you'd find a way to come for me—I thought of the women you'd rescued. The children. How frightened they would be, locked away, unsure of their future, not knowing they had someone championing them. If I didn't have the hope of you…" She trailed off. "That's what kept me from losing it and panicking. I couldn't imagine the terror they would feel. What you do frightens me, Julian, but I understand it a little more. Why it is so important to you."

"It's not as important as you and Jujube are."

"Are you sure?"

I met her eyes. "Yes."

"You could walk away?"

I rubbed my eyes. "As Marcus and Matteo have pointed out, there are others who will take up the fight. They were right when they said, at some point, we all realize we have given all to the cause that we can."

"And you're at that point?"

"Yes, I am."

"Then why are you sending me away?"

"I want to be sure you can forgive me. To give you and Julianna some space. I took that away when I made you stay here, and I won't do that again."

"And if I decide I can't? Will you stay on at Hidden Justice?"

"No."

She didn't say anything, worrying her lip. Julianna

woke up, squirming and blinking, her arms flailing. Tally stood, taking her from my arms. She walked down the hall, disappearing from view, and I felt the beginning of her goodbye in her silence.

I hung my head, defeated and worn, unsure if I had just lost my family.

Later that night, I peeked in on Tally and Julianna. I had paced the apartment, unable to settle. I had so much to say, so many words in my head. I wanted to beg Tally, to make her see how much I needed her and Julianna. But I needed to give her time.

I traced my finger down Julianna's plump cheek, her skin warm and soft under my touch. I glanced over to see Tally watching me. I was shocked when she moved, lifting the covers. I slid in beside her, wrapping her in my arms.

"All right, baby?" I asked quietly.

"I am now. I'm always all right in your arms."

"It's where you belong."

She snuggled closer, and I felt her tears on my chest.

"I'm going to go tomorrow, Julian."

My heart broke, and my voice was thick when I spoke. "Okay, baby. I understand."

"But I want you to come to us as soon as you can."

I pulled back, peering down at her. "What?"

"I'm not the only one who needs to think, Julian. You have to be sure you can give this up—without regrets. I don't want this to come between us."

I began to protest, but she stopped me. "You have to. We both have to be sure."

"I want you. Julianna. A life together."

"I want that too. But I need you to do this."

"How long?" I asked.

"However long it takes."

"I'll miss you, Tally. You and Jujube. I'll miss you so much, and I'll miss more of her growing up." My voice caught. "If you're pregnant——"

"The test was negative. I took it earlier."

I was shocked at the disappointment I felt. But I held her tighter. "We'll work on that later."

"Okay."

I bent my head and kissed her.

"I'll be waiting," she promised.

CHAPTER NINETEEN

Julian

I t took everything in me to watch Tally board that plane with Julianna in her arms. I felt as if a part of me was being ripped away. I had sat and talked to Matteo and Marcus for hours in the dark of the night while my family slept. I was as open and honest as I had ever been with them. They each spoke of their decision, how they made it and why. They also agreed with Tally.

"You need to be sure. Think it through carefully," Matteo advised.

I met Marcus's eyes, and he nodded in understanding. "I know how you feel. When I saw Missy in front of that monster, my decision was made, and I have never wavered. I know your role is different, Julian, but you are still a target—and you know that now. A simple breach in protocol opened you up. It could happen again."

"Close your life here. Come find a new one. There's a spot on the island for you. Tally will have friends, your children will have playmates. A different sort of life, but a good one. Safe. Protected. You can travel, see the world. Help with the fund. Be with your

family. It's a great life." Matteo leaned back. "I have never once regretted my decisions. Evie and our children give me everything I need."

"Thank you for coming to help me get mine back."

Matteo waved me off. "You could have done it without us, but you were right. Marcus walking in threw that asshole off-balance. His little brain couldn't keep up."

Marcus smirked. "I have that effect on people."

We all chuckled, and Matteo became serious. "We'll take care of your family, Julian. Protect them like they are our own. Don't stay away too long."

"I want Tally to have a chance to make sure she wants me in her life."

He gripped my shoulder. "Then we'll see you soon. She is as in love with you as you are with her."

I watched the plane disappear, holding on to those words. Then I left and organized leaving this lonely life.

With Tally safely away, and her permission, I flew to Nova Scotia and stayed in the small, homey cabin that had housed my family and kept them warm and safe. I packed up the personal items I recognized as Tally's and all the baby stuff and shipped it back to Toronto. I spent a full day reading Tally's journal. Pictures she had printed on a cheap color printer that showed her growing stomach. I read of her love for our unborn daughter. Wept at her words of fear and loneliness. Gazed in wonder at her thoughts of the love she held for me. It was there on every page, soaked into the paper.

Some pages were smudged with her tears, mine joining them. I brought it home with me, hoping to relive all those days of discovery as another Jujube grew inside her all over again—this time beside her.

I drove to the small town where June and her aunt lived to deliver the keys and news. I sat and talked to them, the older woman very frail but her strong spirit evident. I assured them both Tally was safe and would always be. I spoke of my love for her and the hope we would weather this storm and be together. I assured her what had torn us apart was resolved, and it seemed to bring her peace.

Cathy patted my hand, her skin pale and delicate against my darker hue. "She has always loved you," she murmured. "She always will. I know you'll find each other again."

I left comforted and at peace. When June let me know her aunt had passed, I sent flowers for her service, feeling a great deal of sadness for her loss, even though I had only met her once. She had loved and protected my family, and I would be eternally grateful.

My boss wasn't shocked when I told him I was done with Hidden Justice. He accepted my resignation with his best wishes for a good life. He understood that the price the agency extracted was high and I had found a different path. I had served them well, and it would carry on without me. My place was elsewhere now.

Regardless of Tally's decision, wherever she was, wherever my daughter was, I would live close. My old life had no place in my new one. My role as father took precedence. My greatest hope was that husband did as well.

A voice clearing brought me out of my musings, and I met Damien's understanding gaze.

"Are you certain?" he asked.

"Yes. You and Leo are the best to run Elite. The two of you will be great faces for the business." Damien had fixed the weak link in the works and hired a group of trusted staff to oversee the system, which was monitored closely twenty-four seven by the most brilliant minds he knew. Protocols, files, and people were under constant surveillance. What occurred with me would never happen again thanks to his talent. He would run the systems for Hidden Justice, but he would not be part of a team. His place would be deep in the shadows so he could find a life outside of the organization and live safely. He deserved that.

Leo spoke up. "Who is taking your place?"

I shrugged. "Top secret. They'll have their own real estate, vision, and teams. I'm technically out of the loop. The building is mine, and I'm leaving it in your hands. Everything to do with Hidden Justice is being moved to the other warehouse so it won't touch you or the business. You can lease the place and add to the profit. I own it in the background, and we split everything the way it's outlined in the documents. You run it as you see fit. Look after the men and take care of them. Elite is a highly profitable and successful endeavor. It will stay that way with you two running it."

"Will you check in?"

"You two will have my information."

Damien watched me with narrowed eyes. "Will Julian Grayson die?"

"No. The Commander will, but not my name. My documents have been altered slightly."

We talked more about the business, I answered any questions, and once we were all satisfied, they got up to leave, shaking my hand. Leo turned at the door.

"Will we see you again?"

For a moment, I was quiet. Then I lifted my hands and shrugged.

"Perhaps. I hope so."

———

I shut the drawer of my desk, looking around. I had very few personal items here. The box I had brought with me was mostly empty. It was much like the apartment before Tally had entered my life. Empty.

She sent me pictures every day. Little notes telling me about Julianna. Assuring me they were fine. The occasional video. I longed for them. I had decided to fly to the island and see them. Talk to Tally face-to-face. Stay somewhere close. I couldn't be separated from either of them anymore. If Tally wasn't ready, I would at least be able to visit Julianna. I knew Tally wouldn't keep me away from her.

My phone buzzed, and I was shocked to see the call came from Tally's cell phone. I answered, feeling anxious.

"Tally?" I asked. "Everything all right?"

"Hi," she murmured. "Everything is good."

I blew out a breath. "Okay. Good."

"It's so beautiful here," she said.

"Yes, it is."

"Peaceful."

"I remember," I told her, wondering if this was leading to something. Her next words surprised me.

"I lied."

"I beg your pardon?"

"Everything isn't good."

"What's wrong, baby?"

"Jujube misses her daddy."

My breath caught. "And her mommy?"

"She misses you too. I need you, Julian. Please come back to us." A sob caught in her voice. "Please."

I stood. "I'm on my way, Tally. Brace yourself, because once I'm there, I'm not leaving."

"I'm counting on it."

"Tell Matteo to start planning that house."

"We already have."

"Fuck," I swore. "I love you, Tally. Kiss Jujube and tell her that Daddy is on his way."

"Matteo said to tell you the jet is at the airport and ready to come back as soon as you are."

"I'll see you tomorrow. Be waiting."

"I will."

She was standing on the sand, Jujube in her arms, as I stepped off the boat that took me over to the island. I rushed toward them, the distance too far, the time since I had last held them too long. The feel of my girls, my family, in my embrace brought a lump to my throat.

The feel of Tally's mouth beneath mine was like coming home. Julianna squirmed, flailing her arms, making little growly noises in her throat. I lifted her high.

"Look how you've grown!" I marveled at her. Her wild hair was longer, redder than it had been, curlier than ever. Her skin was sun-kissed and covered in freckles. She smiled at me—a wide, gummy grin that made me smile with her. I kissed her cheek, blowing a raspberry on it, delighting in her baby giggle, then lifted her again.

Tally held up her hand. "Careful, Daddy, she just—"

Julianna smiled again and puked on me. It hit my shirt, warm and wet, and she giggled again, squirming and impatient. I looked at Tally, who stared back at me, her eyes wide and unblinking.

"Oops," I muttered. "Forgot about that."

Then we were laughing. I tucked Tally under my arm. "Take me home, Tally. I want to change, then sit and look at you for the rest of the day. I've missed your faces."

Later that night, I sat on the beach, listening to the sounds of the waves as they slapped against the shore. I was tired, but I couldn't sleep. It had been busy since I arrived. There was a small guest cottage behind Matteo's house where Tally had been staying, but it offered no privacy today. Everyone came to say hello. Welcome me. Matteo showed me the plans for our house. We had a huge dinner on the patio at Marcus's, the table groaning with food, the laughter and talking nonstop. Through it all, I held Jujube in one arm and Tally's hand with the other. I couldn't stand not being able to touch them.

After dinner, we were finally alone, and I rejoiced in putting Julianna down for bed. She was happy with me, not acting distant at all. Tally and I had talked, but nothing deep or personal. We had time for that. She had fallen asleep on the sofa, and I'd carried her to bed but didn't join her. My mind was too full.

The ocean breeze and the salt air were a heady mix, and I breathed it in greedily. I already envisioned a life here. Time with my girls. Growing our family. Discovering a life not containing violence or fear. No longer being alone.

I heard footsteps, and I looked over my shoulder. Tally approached, her thin nightgown transparent in the moonlight. She began to sit beside me, and I tugged her into my lap so she straddled me.

"You were asleep."

"I woke up, and you weren't there. I thought I had dreamed you being here."

"No, I'm right here, baby. I just couldn't sleep."

She sighed, resting her head on my chest. "It's so lovely here."

"It is." I pushed her heavy hair off her face, kissing her brow. "You're so lovely. I missed you so much, Tally. I never want to be apart from you again."

"Me either."

"Are you sure, Tally? You want me and this life? You'd give up your dreams of being a curator?"

She sighed, gazing up at the stars for a moment. "Dreams change, Julian. And we're so close to so much beauty, so much art and history that I can see and feel for myself. That fills my soul enough—at least for now."

I ran my fingers down her cheek. I knew what she meant. We would build our life together here and let the future happen as it happened. As long as I was with her and Julianna, I had everything I needed.

I held her close for a moment. "Okay, baby."

She shifted and peered up at me. I saw the vulnerability in her eyes. A yearning I hadn't seen before.

"What is it?" I asked.

She sat back, meeting my eyes. "I never want to be away from you either. But you'll have to go back, right?"

"No. I had basically closed everything up already. I was coming to you, Tally. If you weren't ready, I was going to stay close by. I couldn't be without you or Jujube anymore. The few loose ends I can tie up over the internet."

"Good. Because you said you wanted to be around this time."

"This time?" I asked, confused.

"My test was wrong, Julian." She paused. "I'm pregnant."

I stared at her in shock. "Pregnant?" I repeated.

"Yes."

"Is—" I had to swallow. "Is that why you wanted me here? Because you're pregnant?"

"No, I already knew I wanted you here. That I

wanted to share my life with you. This baby is just an added bonus."

I clasped her to me. "Pregnant," I repeated. "And I get to be here this time."

"Yes."

I cupped her face and kissed her. "Every moment, Tally. I will be here every step of the way."

She nodded, tears coursing down her face. "Yes."

"I get another baby to puke and shit all over me at the oddest times."

A laugh escaped her. "Twice the fun."

I enfolded her in my arms. "Twice the love. Ah, Tally, my beautiful wife, thank you."

"You might not be thanking me when I have some odd craving you have to traipse to the mainland for at three in the morning."

"I'll take it."

I held her close, smiling as she fell asleep on me.

Today was the start of my new life. Filled with second chances.

The love of a woman I was crazy about.

A daughter who held my heart in the palm of her tiny hand.

Another child created by the love we shared.

Friends, a new adopted family to share it all with. My own family to watch over.

Any doubts I had about my decision were gone. It was a perfect way to let the Commander go.

Julian the husband, father, and friend would take over.

And I was good with that.

EPILOGUE

Three Years Later

T he water lapped at the shore, long lazy waves that moved at their own pace. The sand was dark from the water, packed firm and solid beneath my feet as I ran. The early morning sun rose slowly, its rays already warm where they touched my face. The island was still asleep, the stillness and beauty that surrounded me, my own little paradise.

I loved this time of the day when I was alone. Soon our little community would be awake and the sounds of the families would echo around me, but for now it was just me. I paused, my hands on my hips as I stared out over the water drinking in the vista I would never tire of.

Endless water, blue sky, and peace. It surrounded me daily.

Love surrounded me.

I glanced toward the house, knowing soon that Jujube would be awake and looking for me. Her baby sister, Skylar, would follow about an hour later. She loved to sleep, that one—my little snuggler.

And Tally, my beautiful wife, would need help to get out of bed and start her day. Close to her due date, she found moving around difficult. The simple act of sitting, laying down, or finding a comfortable position was almost impossible for her at this stage in her pregnancy. She hated it, and although I didn't like seeing her uncomfortable, I still enjoyed seeing every aspect of her pregnancy.

I had immersed myself when she was pregnant with Skylar, every day discovering something new and exciting. The way her body changed, how her curves filled out. The feel of her tummy as it grew to accommodate our child. I loved to talk to it. Read to it. Touch it. I rubbed her back when she was ill, made sure she ate when she could. Supplied her with the endless cravings she had for fresh fruit and cheese croissants. The bakery on the mainland had a standing order I picked up every couple of days.

I reveled in all the new things, panicked over some, while Tally remained calm, having gone through it before. This occasion, I was calmer, but still in awe of her and the entire overwhelming experience we were sharing together. It meant a lot to me. To both of us.

And this time, we were having a boy. A son. I would have been thrilled with another girl, but I had to admit, there was a male ego thing that was secretly happy at the idea of a boy. I wouldn't be so outnumbered now.

I sat down, letting the breeze wash over my face.

This place had healed me. Healed us. I was no longer on guard and vigilant. We were safe here. Tally and my children were safe. I helped with the charter business and worked with Matteo, Marcus, and Gianna on the fund we managed to help victims. I spoke to Damien and Leo on a regular basis and had traveled back to Canada twice to help them with business decisions. But I flew back as quickly as possible, hating to be gone from my world here for long.

I returned back to my family and a life I never dreamed I would live. One filled with love and laughter. Where light and family filled my hours instead of darkness and worry.

A sound caught my ear and I turned, smiling as Tally waddled toward me, holding a cup high as she approached. I stood and went to her, taking the cup and kissing her head.

"You got up without me."

She grimaced. "It wasn't easy, but I did it."

"I didn't expect you up so early. I would have stayed."

She smiled. "Someone is too active for me to sleep."

I rubbed her large belly, bending and kissing the swell. "You're keeping Mommy awake," I tsked. "She needs her rest."

Tally laughed. "I don't think he cares right now. He is too impatient to join us. He's trying to find his way out."

I frowned. "Are you—"

"I think so. I had a few contractions."

I shook my head. My wife was having contractions and made me coffee before walking down to the beach to tell me. "I'll call the midwife."

"I already did. I called Marcus too. He's getting the

boat so she'll be here soon. Missy and Evie are coming to get the girls."

I grasped her hand. "Let's get you to the house."

"No," she replied. "I want to be out here for a while. It feels better when I walk."

I wrapped an arm around her waist. "Lean on me."

She beamed up at me. "I always do."

I kissed her. "My favorite job."

We walked for a bit, her leaning into my side more and more. I heard the sound of the boat leaving. The laughter of my daughters as Missy and Evie came to get them. They brought the girls over for hugs and kisses, Skylar burying her face into my neck as I held her.

"Sweep, Daddy."

I chuckled and kissed her head. She was a mini Tally, right down to the freckles. "You go with Auntie Evie and she'll let you go back to sleep. I'll come get you later, okay?"

"Tay," she mumbled.

Julianna was more aware of what was happening. "The baby coming today?" She asked me.

"I think so."

"Will he be bigger than Skysky was? Can I play with him right away?"

"Not for a bit. But you can hold him."

That satisfied her.

After more kisses and snuggles, they went with Evie and Missy. Without asking, I swooped Tally into my arms. The pained look on her face told me all I needed to know.

"He's coming fast, isn't he?"

"Yes," she ground out. "I hope Marcus hurries."

"I hear the boat. Let's get you inside."

**

Two hours later, I held my son. At just over ten pounds, he was a struggle for Tally, but my brave, incredible wife delivered him. He was long, wrinkled, and red faced as he pushed himself into the world, screaming his displeasure, making us all smile at his entrance.

Once he was cleaned and wrapped, I got him. I stared down at him in wonder, touching the dark hair on his head and stroking his full cheek.

"He's perfect," I said to Tally, who watched us from bed. She was tired and worn out, but still so beautiful.

"He is," she agreed. "And big."

"Strong."

I sat beside her, lifting her hand to my mouth. "Thank you, Tally. For my son. Our girls." I brushed my mouth over hers. "Our life."

"Do you ever regret it?" she asked, sounding vulnerable.

"Giving up Hidden Justice? No. Not a single moment. I love it here. I love our life. Our family." I kissed her again. "I love you."

Our son shifted and I settled him in the crook of my arm. "Matteo once told me his children gave him something he never found in the job. I didn't understand it until I found you. Until you gave me Julianna. Now I get it. Our children, *you*, mean everything to me."

She smiled. "You mean everything to us."

"Then know I have no regrets. I look forward to the rest of my life here with you. I'm sure the kids will keep us plenty busy."

"I'm sure you're right." She sighed as she watched us. "We have to choose a name."

"You still like Joseph?"

"Joseph Alexander Grayson. Joey for short. Yes."

"Then welcome to the world, Joey," I murmured. I heard the sounds of laughter approaching and I grinned.

"Time to meet your sisters. Brace yourself little man."

I stood and gazed at my wife. "Sleep, baby. I'll bring the girls in soon and we can have a family cuddle."

"Sounds good."

I pressed a kiss to her head.

"Yeah, it does."

Thank you so much for reading THE COMMANDER. If you are so inclined, reviews are always welcome by me at your eretailer.

Long ago I had seen a meme circulating romance book groups on social media. Readers asked for the book, and I thought one day. Today is that day.

If you love a possessive alpha hero, Richard and Katy

VanRyan's story begins with my series The Contract. You meet an arrogant hero in Richard, which makes his story much sweeter when he falls.

Enjoy reading! Melanie

ACKNOWLEDGMENTS

Thank you to my wonderful readers who came along for
this ride into Canadian gray.
I hope you enjoyed it!

Lisa—your notes during this series made me smile.
Thank you for your endless patience.
I,love,you,and,thank,you,for,your,comma,lessons.
Pretty,sure,I,nailed,it.

Beth, Trina, Melissa, Carol, and Deb—thank you for
your valuable input, your keen eyes, and
encouragement. Your humor and help are so
appreciated.

Karen—For someone who uses words so much, when it
comes to you there simply
Not enough of them. Thank you, my friend. Love you
to the moon and back.

Kim—You are such a joy. Thank you for being part of
the team and all you do.

My reader group, Melanie's Minions—love you all.

Melanie's Literary Mob—my promo team—you do me proud and I love our interactions.
You are my happy place and I love sharing time with you.
Your support is amazing and humbling.

To all the bloggers, grammers, ticktok-y-ers. Thank you for everything you do. Shouting your love of books—of my work, posting, sharing—your recommendations keep my TBR list full, and the support you have shown me is deeply appreciated.

And my Matthew—my everything. Always. Thank you.

ALSO AVAILABLE FROM MORELAND BOOKS

Titles published under M. Moreland

Insta-Spark Collection

It Started with a Kiss

Christmas Sugar

An Instant Connection

An Unexpected Gift

Harvest of Love

An Unexpected Chance

Following Maggie (Coming Home series)

Titles published under Melanie Moreland

The Contract Series

The Contract (Contract #1)

The Baby Clause (Contract #2)

The Amendment (Contract #3)

Vested Interest Series

BAM - The Beginning (Prequel)

Bentley (Vested Interest #1)

Aiden (Vested Interest #2)

Maddox (Vested Interest #3)

Reid (Vested Interest #4)

Van (Vested Interest #5)

Halton (Vested Interest #6)

Sandy (Vested Interest #7)

Vested Interest Box Set (Books 1-3)

Vested Interest Box Set (Books 4-7)

Vested Interest/ABC Crossover

A Merry Vested Wedding

ABC Corp Series

My Saving Grace (Vested Interest: ABC Corp #1)

Finding Ronan's Heart (Vested Interest: ABC Corp #2)

Loved By Liam (Vested Interest: ABC Corp #3)

Age of Ava (Vested Interest: ABC Corp #4)

Men of Hidden Justice

The Boss

Second-In-Command

The Commander

Mission Cove

The Summer of Us

Standalones

Into the Storm

Beneath the Scars

Over the Fence

My Image of You (Republishing Soon)

Changing Roles

Happily Ever After Collection

Revved to the Maxx

Heart Strings

ABOUT THE AUTHOR

NYT/WSJ/USAT international bestselling author Melanie Moreland, lives a happy and content life in a quiet area of Ontario with her beloved husband of thirty-plus years and their rescue cat, Amber. Nothing means more to her than her friends and family, and she cherishes every moment spent with them.

While seriously addicted to coffee, and highly challenged with all things computer-related and technical, she relishes baking, cooking, and trying new recipes for people to sample. She loves to throw dinner parties, and enjoys traveling, here and abroad, but finds coming home is always the best part of any trip.

Melanie loves stories, especially paired with a good wine, and enjoys skydiving (free falling over a fleck of dust) extreme snowboarding (falling down stairs) and piloting her own helicopter (tripping over her own feet.) She's learned happily ever afters, even bumpy ones, are all in how you tell the story.

Melanie is represented by Flavia Viotti at Bookcase Literary Agency. For any questions regarding subsidiary or translation rights please contact her at flavia@bookcaseagency.com

Connect with Melanie

Like reader groups? Lots of fun and giveaways! Check it out Melanie Moreland's Minions

Join my newsletter for up-to-date news, sales, book announcements and excerpts (no spam). Click here to sign up Melanie Moreland's newsletter

or visit https://bit.ly/MMorelandNewsletter

Visit my website www.melaniemoreland.com

facebook.com/authormoreland

twitter.com/morelandmelanie

instagram.com/morelandmelanie

tiktok.com/melaniemoreland

Printed in the USA
CPSIA information can be obtained
at www.ICGtesting.com
LVHW011619240724
786348LV00015B/897

9 781988 610825